# Lucky John

## Desiree R. Kannel

Black Rose Writing | Texas

ISBN: 978-1-68433-518-3
PUBLISHED BY BLACK ROSE WRITING
www.blackrosewriting.com

Printed in the United States of America
Suggested Retail Price (SRP) $16.95

*Lucky John* is printed in Garamond

*As a planet-friendly publisher, Black Rose Writing does its best to eliminate
unnecessary waste to reduce paper usage and energy costs, while never compromising
the reading experience. As a result, the final word count vs. page count may not meet
common expectations.

Author photo courtesy of Rachael Warecki

# Acknowledgements

I am forever grateful to my daughter, Sarah Rose. She was a teenager when I started this novel and was always patient, loving, and supportive as I spent many nights, early mornings and weekends in front of my laptop, in classes or writing groups.

Another big thank you to the staff and faculty at Antioch University, Los Angeles, including, but not limited to Alma Luz Villanueva, Dana Johnson, Susan Taylor-Chehak, and Tannarive Due. The Universe did an outstanding job sending me there because I also met other newbie writers who would become colleagues and supportive friends.

Thanks to my readers and reviewers: Natalyn Nash, Mercedes Brown, Carollyn Bartosh, Michael Sallwasser, and Karimah Tennyson-Marsh. Your feedback was invaluable!

Finally, I dedicate this book to my father, Mike K. Davis, Jr, who died a few months before publication. Thanks, Daddy. I couldn't have done it without you.

# Lucky John

# Chapter 1

When I called my wife to tell her I was stuck at a meeting in the Valley and wouldn't be home until after nine o'clock, I was lying.

"Big client," I said. "It means a lot to the company and everyone back at the office is depending on me to sign this guy." I called him an asshole too, just so she'd know I wasn't having a good time or something.

She said, "Okay," like she always does and told me to call her when I'm on my way home. Before she hung up, she added that my mother called three times today. "She wants to know when you're coming to see your father." I told Pamela I would call my mom later to make the arrangements. My second lie.

I lied for the same reason that most husbands lie to their wives: I was having an affair. And not my first affair, or my first lie. But it is not important what number in the queue this one affair happened be. What is important is that this one turned out to be my last.

Before I called Pamela, I had a call from Kim, and she informed me that she had some free time that evening, and would I be interested in getting together to go over my sales last month? I was on the freeway driving away from that meeting, and someone was listening on her side because she used her business voice— talking like I was one of her Sally Anne Cosmetics clients. After almost a year of Kim, I had her little code-talk down, so I played along. I told her that I would love to go over my sales record with her.

"In about an hour? At that little coffee shop on PCH?" No problem. I called Pamela right after that, and then turned my car towards the Sea View Motel on Pacific Coast Highway.

Twenty minutes later, when I got to the motel, she was already there. Her red Mustang convertible was parked in the farthest corner away from the street. Her safe spot. Kim's husband is an asshole, but a very rich one, and she wasn't about to throw it all away by getting caught. And that's one of the reasons I picked her.

1

I wouldn't have to worry about her turning into another Jessica. That one, which should have been my last, turned into a nightmare with late-night phone calls, hang-ups, and drives by the house during dinner time. I even caught her spying on us at church one Sunday. And she's not even Methodist. When I confronted her, she said it's a free country and she could go to any church she wanted. I took Pamela and Jackson home. The next Sunday, Pamela said she had a headache so we didn't go. She had a lot of Sunday morning headaches that year, and we never returned to that church.

When Kim let me in the room, she was on her cell phone; her face all scrunched up and angry. "I told you that I would take care of it tomorrow," she said. She was also smoking in a nonsmoking room, so I motioned for her to put it out. She rolled her eyes at me and kept on talking. "Allison, we can get it tomorrow. Mr. Spivey will understand if you don't have it yet."

Her daughter. She would be awhile, so I stepped over to the dresser and unbuttoned my shirt. I took the change out of my pocket and checked out the quarters—two Californias, one Maine, three New Yorks, and one Minnesota. This made me smile. Jackson and I started coin collecting about a year ago after I picked up one of those state quarter collection booklets. I was on a business trip and saw it in the airport gift shop. It was a big picture of the United States folded in half, made of cardboard. Each state had a hole in it to put the quarter in, and each night I would empty my pockets and we'd search through the change together; our father-son bonding time. I had to do something. He was home all day with his mother, doing god-knows-what, and I would come home and my kid would practically ignore me. I'd tell him to go wash for dinner and he'd turn to his mom—like he needed her approval before moving. It was getting to me, but then Terry, that next one after Jessica, suggested that I find something he and I could do together. "Make it something special—just between father and son." She was a child psych major, and I figured a little free advice couldn't hurt, so I took it. She had suggested a sport like baseball or soccer, but that meant evening practices and weekend games, plus Pamela hadn't liked the idea too much. Jackson was born a few weeks premature and needed to spend about a month at the hospital before we brought him home. Five years later, she still calls him fragile and won't let him do anything she feels is too strenuous. When I saw that coin collecting booklet in the gift shop at the Las Vegas airport, I bought it thinking we could do our bonding over a bunch of quarters. Nothing too strenuous about that.

Kim hung up her phone and dropped it on the nightstand. She continued going on about Allison and school and teachers having unreasonable demands. "Those fucking people act like parents have nothing better to do than to run around town getting shit for those stupid projects."

I looked at her. The furthest thing from my mind was getting into a discussion about that kid. It was almost six, and Pamela expected me home around eight. Two hours is plenty of time, but not if we spent one of them debating the faults of the educational system.

I needed to change the subject, so I said, "Check this out. I found a Minnesota quarter. Jackson and I have been searching for one of these for months." I smiled at her, remembering what my kindergarten teacher used to say about smiles being contagious. It didn't work. She gave me another eye roll, shook her head, and said she had to go pee.

She emerged from the bathroom in a better mood and ready to get at it. I knew this because she was completely naked. She told me that we didn't have much time because she needed to take her daughter to get what she called some special, bullshit graph paper for geometry.

"With all the taxes we have to pay," she said, getting into bed, "you'd think they could buy the goddamn paper."

I sat on the side of the bed with my shirt half unbuttoned and looked over at her. She was lying on her side, her head propped up by her arm. Her blond hair pulled back into a single ponytail exposed a half-inch of black roots that circled her face, almost making it look like she was wearing a headband. The only make-up she wore was some dark red lipstick, and I handed her a tissue to wipe it off. She reached for it and started singing that song about lipstick on collars, perfume, and the want ads. Kim is white, and this was her way of trying to bridge the racial thing between us. Things like singing old Motown songs or talking about some Terry McMillan book she read with her bookclub; like I gave a damn about those things.

She got into that song and started throwing her head and shoulders back and forth so much that her silicon-filled breasts jiggled like a pair of water balloons pinned to a piece of plywood, just waiting for some lucky kid to hit one with a dart. I pointed to her chest and told her she needed to stop before one of them popped or broke loose or something. She cupped her hands around her breasts and said that they had better not after what she paid for them. She moved her thumb back and forth across those pink nipples and gazed up at me, trying to be sexy, but it wasn't working. Kim was ten years older than me, and the lines on her face were really showing. Maybe it was the lighting in that cheap motel room, or the irritation from talking with her kid hadn't worn off yet, but looking into that pasty face with the smeared off lipstick and wrinkles that had never bothered me before lead to a total turn off. Making love to her would take a lot more effort and acting than I had the strength or patience for. I started thinking of a way to get out of the room.

I glanced at the clock on the night stand, shook my head and told her there wasn't enough time. She insisted there would be plenty of time—if I would just hurry up. She turned the covers down on my side of the bed and patted the mattress. Her bracelets jingled together, sounding like loose change.

The idea to call my son came, which meant telling him a lie, but I was stalling for time with Kim and felt that the benefits outweighed the little white lie. I reached inside my pants pocket and took out my phone. When she asked me what I was doing, I told her I needed to call Jackson to tell him something.

"Tell him when you get home. I told you we don't have that much time," she said. It sounded like an order.

Wanting an argument so I could get out of there, I shot back how *I* waited while she talked to her kid, so she could just wait while I called my son.

"What's so important that it has to be right now?" she asked.

"None of your business," I said, since I did not want to tell her about the quarters. I knew she would laugh and say something about how high school geometry was more important than coin collecting. Turned out I didn't have to worry about getting into it with her anyway because her phone vibrated on the night stand. She caught it just before it slid off the side. It was Allison again. She wanted to know if her mom was on her way home. Kim gave me the, *are we or aren't we* face. I ignored her and turned away to call Jackson.

She let out an exaggerated sigh and said, "Yeah, honey. I'm just leaving now."

She got up, mumbling the whole time about how maybe it (meaning me) just wasn't worth her time anymore. I kept quiet and watched as she threw her designer clothes back on and fixed her make up. Our rendezvous were beginning to look a lot like my home life—too much bitching and not enough sex. So, what was the point?

After Kim left, I sat on the edge of the bed and called my house.

"I thought you were in a meeting." Pamela said meeting the same way she tells her name to people, accent on every syllable—mee-ting. I told her we were on a short break and asked to speak to Jackson.

"He's watching TV."

"Just put him on the phone. I have a surprise for him." I heard her calling him and after half a minute he came on the line.

"Dad?" he said. I could hear cartoons in the background. I told Jackson to turn the TV off. "Mom says I can still watch," he said.

"Just turn it off," I shouted into the phone. I worried about him. He would be deaf before he hit puberty, and I was the only one who seemed to care. It's also turning him into a loner. Pamela lets him watch too much TV, and he never wants to go outside to play with the other kids.

When he came back on, I told him about my find. He asked me where I got it from. "What does that matter?" I answered. "When I get home, we can fill that hole in Minnesota."

"Tommy Green's dad just goes to the bank and gets them," Jackson said. "They had a whole roll of Minnesotas. We could've had one of theirs. His dad said it was okay."

Tommy Green's dad is a jack-ass. "What's the fun in that?" I said. "Any fool can walk into a bank and get them. That's the lazy man's way to do it." I rolled my eyes thinking about that family. Ever since they moved in across the street, it's been let's keep up with the Joneses around our house. Pamela was always talking about how the Greens did this, or bought that, or traveled there for vacation. The last thing a working man needs is some over achieving do-gooder living across the street, reminding your wife and kid how inadequate you are.

"Mom wants to know when your mee-ting will be over." I told him to tell her we were almost finished, but not to expect me for another hour or so. He said Mom wanted to talk to me, but I told him I had to get back and hung up before she came on the line.

"Did he call your grandmother?" I heard her asking about my mom right before I hung up. No, I didn't, and I wasn't going to tonight. Mom and Dad went to bed early. At least they had before. I really didn't know how their lives had changed since the stroke. Bobby called me right after it happened, and he was pissed that I hadn't dropped everything and gone home. It had been almost a year since I'd been home, so they could wait a few more weeks.

After I left the hotel room, I stood in front of my car, keys in hand, wondering what to do to pass the time. I wanted to catch Jackson right at his bedtime which meant getting home at 8:00. I was fifteen minutes from home, and there was a Denny's across the street, so I decided that would be a good enough place to wait.

The restaurant had that quiet-after-the-storm feel. Most of the tables were empty but still had dirty dishes on them, and a couple of cooks were sitting at the counter drinking coffee. Their aprons were filthy. I had passed two waitresses and a busboy taking a smoke break outside the front door. The younger waitress had her shoes off and was rubbing her feet. I hoped she would think to wash her hands before clocking back in.

After waiting too long for a table, I decided to sit at the counter. The cooks had left, and I sat down in between two empty stools that still had the previous diners' dishes on the counter. Someone hadn't finished their tuna melt and fries. After I ordered a coffee, the busboy from outside came by, cleared the dishes, and left new place settings. Before he walked away, I exchanged my dirty spoon for a clean one. I looked around and saw the feet-rubbing waitress coming out of the bathroom. When I walked past her outside, I couldn't see her face because she was bent over concentrating on her aching feet. When she turned towards me, my head snapped back in surprise. Hers did the same.

I felt like I was stuck inside a slow-motion movie as I sat there, mouth hanging open staring at Janet Moore, who was staring right back at me. Her hair was longer than I remembered, and she had lost some weight too. The waitress uniform she wore looked about two sizes too big for her, and she was wearing glasses. I didn't remember glasses, but the eyes behind the glasses were the same. Bright and dark brown with long lashes and slanted just enough to make her look like an ethnic mystery. The kids in our neighborhood used to tease her by calling her offensive names. They would use their fingers to pull their own eyes back while talking in funny accents. They only stopped when her older brothers began threatening everyone. I asked her once if it bothered her. She told me she usually ignored them.

Our trance dissolved when the other waitress came back and asked if I was ready to order. Without taking my eyes of Janet, I told her all I wanted was coffee.

"Is that all?" She rapped her pen against the pad. I murmured a yes without taking my eyes off Janet.

She must have been a manager or something because she told Janet that her break was over and to go check on table number fourteen. Like a robot, Janet turned away from me and walked towards a table where a family of five had just sat down. I ignored my waitress as she freshened up my coffee and let my eyes follow Janet to table fourteen. She was still beautiful, even as tired as she seemed that night. I wanted her to come back so I could check her left hand, and I assumed she would come back, if only to say hi.

I watched her take the drink orders, but it looked like the littlest kid couldn't make up his mind. He threw a fit about something his mother told him. Janet just stood before them, pad and pen in hand, rocking back and forth on her feet. She was wearing cheap shoes, not at all the right shoes for a waitress. No wonder her feet were bothering her. If she was married, he was a cheap son of a bitch not to buy his wife a decent pair of working shoes.

It was hard for me to imagine Janet married. She was just fourteen when I left, and in my mind she had never aged. I did a quick calculation in my head and figured she would be going on thirty-one by now. Three years younger than me. If she was married, I hoped it wasn't to that Eric Baker. But then I thought that would explain those shoes because I could just picture his fat, cheap, lazy ass sitting at home in front of the TV watching reruns of *Battlestar Galactica* while his wife limped around waiting tables in cheap shoes.

One of the few letters I got from home while I lived with Aunt Idell was a newspaper clipping of Janet at her coming-out ball. Baker was her escort, and from the picture it looked like his mom had had to use a crow bar to stuff his big butt into that tux. Janet didn't looked very happy standing next to him. Aunt Idell said she was probably just nervous because she was the center of attention that night. To me it was just a stupid dance, and it wasn't until I met Pamela that I understood how important those balls were to some Black families. But when I looked into my Janet's eyes, I knew it wasn't nerves that made her look that way. I was sure she had been wishing that I was there instead of Eric Baker.

That kid at table fourteen must have made up his mind because Janet started making her way back to the counter where the coffee pots and drinks were. Before filling their order, she came and stood in front of me, hands in her pockets.

She looked me right in the eyes and said, "Hello John. Long time, no see."

I laughed when she said that, *long time*. I told her seventeen years was a long time. She looked confused and asked me if it had really been that long. I couldn't tell if she was serious or not, so I just shrugged my shoulders because I didn't want her to think I had been counting the years like they mattered or something. I took a sip of coffee and prayed my hand wasn't shaking.

"How long have you been working here?" I needed to change the subject.

This was only her second month. She said with her mom passed on, and her dad running off with that nurse, she didn't see any reason to stay in town anymore. I had no idea what she was talking about, but I just nodded and gave what I hoped was an understanding smile. I figured my mother must still pretend to everyone back home that all is fine with us, so of course Janet would think I would be up-to-date with everything and everyone from the old neighborhood. Before she turned away to fill that drink order, she asked, "How is your dad doing? Jeff and Jamal told me about the stroke."

Ice cubes clinked together as she prepared the drink order. As she worked, I watched her shoulder blades rotate back and forth under her uniform. I couldn't answer her question, so I didn't, and waited for her to walk back to table fourteen. I looked at my watch. It was almost 7:30. I wanted to ask what time she got off, or if she worked every Thursday night, but I couldn't. She had assumed I knew all about what had been going on in her life, but I needed to know how much of my life she might (or might not) have heard about. My mom tended to either exaggerate or just plain make things up to fill in the gaps. And since we rarely talked, there were a lot of gaps to fill.

When Janet came back, I stood up and read the bill. Janet took it from my hand and said it was on her.

"A gift between old friends," she smiled.

I smiled back and said, "Only if you'll let me repay the favor sometime." She was looking at me with those eyes, trying to figure out if I was flirting with her, but she didn't seem to mind if I was.

The waitress-manager came by and gave her a get back to work look, so she took my bill and shoved it in her pocket. No ring. I raised my eyebrows at her, letting her know I was waiting for an answer.

She smiled and said, "That would be great. I would love to meet your wife and little Jackson."

Good old mom, I thought as I threw some change on the counter. I didn't want Janet to have to pay the tip for that sorry-ass waitress.

On the drive home, I let the image of a fourteen-year-old Janet morph into the woman in the waitress uniform. It was easy because she hadn't changed that much. She was older but didn't really look older, just looked tired. After what she told me, I could see why. I tried to piece together a complete picture with the few details she had mentioned. The new woman in her dad's life might have been the nurse they hired to take care of their mom. Or maybe she had worked at the pharmacy with Jeff and Jamal. Whoever she was, Mr. Moore must have gotten too old to worry about keeping up appearances. I guess you can teach an old dog new tricks, especially if the teacher happens to have a great pair of legs and no scruples. I wondered if he left before or after the funeral.

Jeff and Jamal were Janet's older twin brothers. I knew that because they used to be my best friends. We were all the same age, and I started hanging out with them in junior high after I left the baseball team. Jeff and Jamal didn't play any sports—their dad used to say that he was grooming them for better things, which meant taking over the family drug store. We used to hang out together so much that people began calling us the 3-Jays. Kind of like that singing group. We didn't sing, though. We just hung out, and once in a while Jamal would steal some old lady's prescription and we'd waste an afternoon daring each other to swallow the pills. One time, we wrapped some little pink pills in tuna fish and fed them to the neighbor's cat. After Snowball died, Jamal stopped stealing pills.

The last time I talked to Janet was also the last time I talked to the twins. I did know that their father's grooming had paid off. Jamal was the store's manager and Jeff the pharmacist. They had two stores in Crown City. Janet's aversion to the family business must have stuck. But a waitress?

Fifteen minutes later, I surprised myself as I pulled into my driveway. I sat for a few seconds and had that eerie feeling drivers get when they seem to operate on a sort of autopilot. I couldn't remember one thing about that drive home. Did I run any red lights? Did I signal all my turns? Did I hit anybody? I looked in the rearview mirror, expecting to see at least one police car, lights flashing. The street was clear. I took a deep breath and thanked the driving gods for getting me home in one piece.

The sound of cartoons and Jackson's laughter greeted me at the front door. I yelled that I was home, put my briefcase on the entry table and walked to the family room. Jackson, dressed in his Spider Man pajamas, was on the couch, eyes glued to the screen. I walked in and turned off the TV.

"Hey! Mom says I have an extra fifteen more minutes tonight." He protested.

Pamela must have heard him because she came in from I don't know where and asked him what was wrong. He pointed at me the same way witnesses point at that unlucky suspect in a line-up. Pamela glared at me and asked why I turned off the TV.

"He's been watching TV all day. It isn't going to kill him to turn it off fifteen minutes early," I said.

She put her hands on her hips and told me that, "For your information, he hadn't been watching TV all day," and that she gave him fifteen extra minutes because he ate all his vegetables at dinner.

"You shouldn't bribe a kid to eat his vegetables," I said.

She moved her hands from her hips and crossed her arms. "Tell me, Dr. Spock," she said. "What would you have done, had-you-been-here?" During that last part, her head did that bobbing from side-to-side thing. Sort of like a dance to match the sarcasm in her voice.

I told her that all I wanted to do was spend some time with my son before he went to sleep. "I've-been-working-all-day," I told her, bobbing my head from side to side too. Sometime during our little exchange, Jackson had sneaked behind me and turned the TV back on. Pamela unfolded her arms and let them drop to her side. She told him to turn it off.

"Your father wants to spend some quality time with you." She walked out of the room.

My son turned off the TV and stood at my side, waiting for this quality time to begin. I looked down at him, and Pamela's round, dark eyes stared back at me. I asked him how his day at school went.

"Fine," he answered.

"Did you have any homework?"

"No."

"Did you play with Tommy today?"

"No."

I started to panic. Jackson was only five-years-old, and I was already running out of things to talk with him about. He had become the king of the one-word response. Terry had told me that this was typical behavior for this age and that he would grow out of it soon. She advised me to stay calm and not rush him, so I put my hands in my pockets and waited for him to engage. I got my reward a few seconds later when Jackson grabbed my hand and asked me about the Minnesota.

"That's right," I said, excited and relieved. "Where's the folder?" He kept it in his bedroom, and I carried him upstairs on my shoulders, treating him like he just scored the winning touchdown. Pamela appeared in his doorway to see what all the noise was about. Jackson retrieved the booklet from under his bed while I reached in my pocket and pulled out the change. Among the nickels, dimes and pennies, I had one California, and two New Yorks. I took a deep breath and closed my eyes while my mind raced back to the counter at Denny's, and I saw my hand throwing a few faceless coins on the counter.

Jackson had the booklet open on his bed. He pointed to the empty spot for the Minnesota coin and said, "Now we're all caught up, Dad. Do you know what state's coming out next?" He sounded really excited.

Pamela was watching me from the doorway. When I didn't answer my son, she told him to go brush his teeth and get ready for bed.

"But what about the Minnesota?"

She came into the room, put her arm around his shoulders and guided him into the bathroom.

"We'll ask the Greens tomorrow if they have any left," she said just before I heard the water faucet come on.

# Chapter 2

My wife's name is Pamela, not Pam. She used to be okay with Pam, but after that cooking spray became a household name, the teasing started. Her last name was Sprey. No kidding. She said the teasing was awful and to stop it she just told everyone to call her Pamela instead of Pam. I guess it worked because she never went back. Her family thought that after we got married, she would be all right with Pam again since it's a lot harder to make a joke out of Pam Roberts. But she wouldn't go back. She said that it had been so long with everyone calling her Pamela, she didn't think she could respond to just Pam.

My father-in-law is the Sprey family patriarch and historian. It didn't take me long to realize that because unlike my own, the Spreys are a proud and solid family, bonded to a history that Mr. Sprey keeps alive.

Their story begins in St. Paul, Minnesota. That's where Pamela's great-grandfather, Caleb Jackson, moved to after he left his family's farm, located somewhere near Huntsville, Alabama. The year was 1900, and he let his family know that he wasn't going to spend any part of the new century picking nothing, so one morning before the sun came up and the okra was ripe, he just up and left the farm, his family, and Alabama. And he never looked back. No one knows how he got there. There wasn't money for trains or steamboats, so he probably walked most of the way. He wouldn't have tried to hitch. Back then, that would have been like hanging a sign around his neck saying: LYNCH ME. Whatever he did, it was enough, and in the spring of 1901 his momma got a letter from him saying he'd made it to St. Paul, and that's where he planned on living for the rest of his life. In all that time, his people in Huntsville got one more letter from him, which was right after Pamela's grandmother was born.

So there's Caleb Jackson, fresh from the country and determined to make it in the big city. Common sense lead him to where he saw other Black folks living and working, but that turned out to be a mistake. Caleb Jackson was used to the bigotry and nastiness of the whites back home, but the big surprise was receiving that same treatment from his own people. To those St. Paul Negroes, Caleb Jackson was just a dirty, uneducated and uncivilized country boy. The head waiter at the St. Paul Hotel wouldn't even talk to him about a job. Said the people at the St. Paul had no time for some country hick who couldn't tell a soup spoon from his own dick. The only people who would talk to him about work were at the slaughterhouses, and that's where he ended up. Caleb Jackson traded the hot sun of the open fields for the cold, dank smell of blood and death. And that pleased him just fine.

Back home in Huntsville, a white man named Mr. Thomas would come by the house two times a year after the family cleared the fields. Mr. Thomas would take most of the crop, all of Caleb's daddy's money, and then his momma would cry and worry about how they were going to make it until the next growing season. Caleb Jackson never understood how a man who worked so hard could end up having so little. His family didn't own that farm; Mr. Thomas did, and it was his to take back and kick them out anytime he felt like it. That's a hard threat to hold over a man, and Caleb Jackson swore he would never get caught that way. After three years of sweating in that cold slaughterhouse, killing cows and cutting them up into little pieces, Caleb Jackson put $250 down on a three bedroom, two-story house, and took his first step toward respectability in the eyes of the Negro population of St. Paul.

After he had the house, Caleb Jackson knew what his next step needed to be. He married a woman named Charlotte—not the first woman he asked, but the first to say yes. Charlotte had one quarter Indian mixed in with her St. Paul Negro blood, so it was generally accepted that marrying a country boy wasn't too much of a step down. The two of them spent the next seven years paying on the house and having babies. By 1911, they had four boys, all of them with dark brown skin, black curly hair, and flat noses. Caleb used to tease his wife and say his African blood had scared away her little bit of Dakota blood.

A girl would have been nice, but after Little Henry was born the doctor told Caleb to stay away from his wife because she wouldn't live through another pregnancy. The doctor told him that he would just have to be content with his boys. And he was, for a while.

That slaughterhouse job soon turned out to be an inadequate source of income for a family of six, so Caleb took up work wherever he could get it. He chopped and hauled wood in the winter. In the summer, they let him do kitchen work at the St. Paul Hotel, but made him stay away from the guests. The head cook told him the stink from the slaughterhouse would make the white folks sick. When the oldest boy, Robert, turned seven, Caleb got him a job delivering newspapers before school. He and Charlotte even set up a little garden in back of their house and sold extra vegetables to the neighbors. Charlotte and the kids did most of the outdoor work; Caleb Jackson set the prices and collected the money. They grew everything but okra.

In 1915, Caleb Jackson paid the last twenty-five dollars owed on the house. After the man at the bank gave him the deed, he strutted home carrying that deed like it was the Declaration of Independence. Caleb Jackson walked down the street his house was on, and he walked through his front yard and up his porch steps. He opened up his front door, stood in his threshold and looked at his family. The boys were running down the stairs, out the front door, right past their daddy and down to the lake for a swim. His wife came in from the back carrying a basket of his clean laundry. As soon as she saw him, she knew. Her husband worked harder than any man she had ever known, and there he stood with his reward rolled up in hands that reeked of blood no matter how hard he scrubbed them.

Right after they were married, and before the babies starting coming, Caleb would lie next to his wife after the lovemaking and share stories about the white men in Huntsville coming around after all the crops were in and everybody worn out.

"Every year it was the same. Daddy would load up the wagon with all that cotton, and Mister Thomas would come and haul it away, talking about how we still owed him money 'cause the price of cotton was low or the cost of supplies high. It was always one thing or another keeping my daddy from owning that farm outright."

"Shouldn't you have stayed on to help?" Charlotte whispered.

Caleb Jackson laughed and told his wife that staying on to help wouldn't have done nothin' for nobody. "Daddy could've had Jesus Christ, Himself, fly down from Heaven and work them fields right alongside him and my brothers. That wouldn't have made not one bit a difference to Mister Thomas and them white folks down there. End of season, they would come 'round, just like always, haul it all away, leaving us no better off than we was before *and* with an extra mouth to feed through the winter."

Standing there in his house, holding that deed in his fist, Caleb Jackson knew for sure that there would be no white man coming round telling him to get out. And no more St. Paul Negroes looking down on him, neither. Caleb Jackson, country boy from Huntsville, Alabama, had come up to St. Paul, Minnesota and did in ten years what his daddy and brothers would never be able to do. Never.

Caleb Jackson looked at his wife and knew there was only one more thing he needed to make this day, his Independence Day, complete. Besides, how was some doctor going to tell him what he could or couldn't do with his own wife? In his own home?

She knew what was on his mind, so she put the laundry basket down at the foot of the steps and walked up to their bedroom. Before he followed her, Caleb Jackson placed his deed in the top drawer of the little desk that sat in the front room. No one saw it again until after he died. His oldest grandson found it when they came to clean out the house for the new owners. Isaiah told his father that the yellowing piece of paper smelled like rotting meat.

After they laid Pamela's great-grandmother to rest, Caleb Jackson sat down and wrote his second letter to Huntsville. He told his sister that his wife had died and left him four boys and a newborn baby girl named Rose. He wrote that his daughter looked just like his wife and asked his sister to come live with him to help him raise his baby girl, her niece. He told her that St. Paul was hot in the summer and cold in the winter, that his boys were good boys who minded well, and he put ten dollars in the envelope and asked her to write him back telling them when to expect her.

Down in Huntsville, it was common knowledge that Hattie Lee hated farming almost as much as her older brother had. But since she was a girl, walking away from the farm wasn't much of an option, and her other options weren't looking too good neither. She was twenty-five and had turned away three suitors. They were farmers, and Hattie Lee was not interested in marrying a dirty farmer. Her daddy whooped her each time she said no, but that hadn't changed her mind. She told him she'd rather get whooped than marry a farmer. When Caleb's letter came, Mr. Jackson knew he would miss his daughter, but he also knew that there wasn't any good reason to keep her in Huntsville anymore. He wasn't interested in having to feed and clothe a grown woman who thought she was too good to marry his neighbors' sons. Caleb was welcome to have her.

After his sister arrived, Caleb Jackson stopped parenting his children, and Hattie Lee took to St. Paul like she was born there. Not long after she stepped down off that train, Hattie Lee dropped her southern accent, pressed her hair, wore white gloves in the summer, and used her niece's light skin and good hair as her calling card into the all the finer Negro establishments in St. Paul. Under her auntie's guidance, Rose Jackson grew into the kind of sister that's hard to like. Just like her Aunt Hattie, Rose grew up thinking herself better than, and too good for her own people.

•          •          •

The first time I met Pamela's Grandma Rose was on an Easter Sunday about four months after we started dating. She lived in one of those assisted-living homes called Peaceful Horizons. Their lobby looked like one you'd see in a five-star resort, complete with a concierge. Pamela's grandmother had her own suite on the third floor; a simple, small one-bedroom apartment with a tiny kitchenette and bathroom, complete with all the necessary handicap accessories. The kitchen was only for show—a way to make the residents feel like they had normal apartments and lived normal lives. The stove didn't work for fear of burns, and the refrigerator was used to keep her insulin and Ensure cold. There was always a nurse or aide coming by to check on her, and their meals were served in a large dining hall on the first floor.

That's where we all had Easter dinner, her parents (whom I had already met), her brother and his wife, their two kids, and a young cousin from Alabama who had come out to California in the fall to go to UCLA. His name was Lee Jackson.

The dining room was packed, and I had never seen so many walkers, electric wheelchairs, and portable oxygen tanks all in one place before. While waiting in the buffet line, some old guy kept bumping his wheelchair into me. Thinking it was my fault, I said excuse me each time and tried to get out of his way. But he kept following me, ramming that wheelchair into my back. When Pamela's dad began laughing and pointing at us, I realized that the old guy was doing it on purpose. It was his way of welcoming newcomers to the Peaceful Horizons Assisted Living Community. When I got back to our table with a plate of low-sodium ham and fat-free mashed potatoes, the whole family had a good laugh at my expense. I looked at Pamela, but she wasn't joining in on the joke. I think she worried about what my reaction would be, or maybe that I would say the wrong thing. Truth was, I was more embarrassed than mad, so I let them have their fun and even joined in after a while. Later, when we were alone, she put her arms around my neck and thanked me for being such a good sport. Her voice was soft and sexy, and her eyes looked straight into mine. I liked it when she talked to me that way because there was no bullshit or sarcasm in her voice.

I kissed her and said, "No problem."

Since I had already met Pamela's parents (and since I didn't want to hear any more about the wheelchair incident) I spent most of that afternoon talking with Grandma Rose. Her skin was light colored; a shade that caused curious eyes to linger and ill-mannered people to ask. She was wearing a lavender dress with matching shoes and had a small white purse on her lap. She talked a lot about growing up in St. Paul, her daddy who ignored her, her brothers who treated her like the family pet, and her Aunt Hattie.

"If it hadn't been for Aunt Hattie, I would have been raised a savage, just like my brothers were. Aunt Hattie tried to teach them right, but they were too hard-headed." In between sips of tea, she told me that her aunt had taught her all she needed to know about being a lady and how to tell respectable society from trash.

Hattie spent Caleb Jackson's money on private schools for Coloreds, piano lessons, dance recitals, etiquette lessons, and the big event: her debutante ball. That was back in the summer of 1932, but Grandma Rose could describe her gown, with the yards and yards of pink satin and lace like it was hanging upstairs in her closet. Whenever she talked about that dress, her hands would rise to her shoulders, then glide down her sides and flare out around her knees—just like she was running those eighty-nine-year-old hands over her sixteen-year-old body, all dressed up and ready to show St. Paul her respectable and cultured self.

That ball was the highlight of the Negro society in St. Paul, and Aunt Hattie had made up her mind that her niece was going. None of the other families would allow their sons to accompany the daughter of a man who killed cows for a living, so they settled on the youngest son of the cook at the hotel where Caleb worked part time.

Seventy years later, Grandma Rose could describe her gown down to the color of the buttons on the back. She could name who was there, what they wore, and who they went home with. She could describe the ballroom with the red and white flower centerpieces, and the patterns on the china, yet she could not tell me the name of the boy who had escorted her.

"I think his name was Paul or Pat or something that starts with a P," she said. "He did give me a lovely white and pink rose corsage, though. I pressed it into my Bible as soon as I got home."

Grandma Rose's life must have ended the night of her début because that's where her stories ended. Everything else I know about her I learned from Pamela and her family. Sometimes told to me, sometimes putting bits of talk or gossip together. Turns out the son of that cook gave Rose more than a corsage that night, because a few months later, Caleb Jackson was banging on the father's house demanding that Paul or Pat or whoever marry his daughter. Caleb was pissed. Not at Rose, but at his sister. Claimed she didn't do a good enough job looking after his daughter and all she did was waste his money on lessons and fancy dresses, and the only thing he could see coming out of it was a knocked-up, stuck-up girl that nobody wanted to marry. Not even the boy who did it. However, there was a man working at the slaughterhouse who was known for being slow. His son was even slower, so it didn't take much for Caleb Jackson to convince him to marry his Rose. The two hundred dollar dowry helped a lot too. After a quick wedding, the newlyweds headed out to Los Angeles, where Rose's new husband, Butler Sprey, had a job waiting for him working the railroads. They say he worked on Union Station, but that's just a rumor. What was a fact was that he was slow in the head. Rose had to take care of all the family's money and business. Butler didn't do much except bring home a paycheck once a month. And apparently, his slowness was confined to the upper part of his body. After Little Butler, Pamela's dad, was born, Rose Sprey got in the family way six more times. She lost two of them, leaving Pamela with one uncle and two aunts.

Pamela's father is a junior—Butler Sprey, Jr., which makes his nickname, and the name that most call him, BJ. BJ Sprey.

I always call him, Mr. Sprey.

# Chapter 3

The morning after I saw Janet at the Denny's was a Friday. Pamela was up before me and had taken Jackson to her family's place in Baldwin Hills in South Los Angeles. They would be there until late Sunday. It was the first anniversary of Grandma Rose's death. She had turned ninety-five on a Tuesday and then died a week later. Folks silently agreed that it was the big birthday celebration that did her in. Everyone was there: family from California, St. Paul and even Huntsville. A good time was had by all and Rose, dressed all in pink and satin, had never looked happier.

When I finally rolled out of bed, there was a note from my wife on the nightstand reminding me to call my mom. I didn't need reminding. I had decided to call first thing in the morning. I would have to talk about Dad's condition for a few minutes before I could casually slide in seeing Janet at the Denny's. That drop of info would be all my mother would need to spill the details about our old neighbors, the Moores.

I used the bedside phone to make the call. After three rings, a deep female voice picked up and said hello.

"Mom?"

"Bobby?" the voice answered. "I thought you were with your mother."

"This is John," I told the voice. "Who is this?"

The voice laughed. "Oh, John." More laughter. "Your mamma has been trying to get in touch with you. She'll be real sorry she missed your call." Another laugh. "My goodness, don't you sound just like your brother."

I was getting impatient, so I repeated my earlier question: "Who are you?"

The voice must have sensed the tension because the laughter stopped. "I'm Mrs. Anderson. Your daddy's aide."

"Aide? You mean like a nurse?"

"No. I'm a home care aide. Your mother is with Bobby, looking at homes."

"Homes?"

It was her turn to be impatient. "Nursing homes. For your father."

I shut my eyes tight and tried to take that in. Mrs. Anderson took my silence as a request to keep talking, so she told me all about how it had been a hard decision for my mom to make, but that the doctors thought it was the best thing for everyone involved.

"Especially Mrs. Roberts," she said. "Taking care of your daddy, a man in his condition, would be too much for her." Then she told me that that was why she had been trying to reach me. "I guess she wanted your opinion on the home."

I mumbled something about how work's been really busy with… stuff.

Mrs. Anderson suggested I call Bobby on his cell phone, but I got out of that by saying I didn't want to bother them. That seemed to satisfy her, so I hung up right after saying thanks. The truth was that I didn't have his cell number, and I didn't want her to have to tell me that, too.

The last time I talked to Bobby was when he called from the payphone at the hospital emergency room.

"Dad had a stroke," he had shouted over the noise. "Mom wants you to come home right away." After I asked how bad off Dad was, Bobby got angry and told me that it didn't matter how bad, or good, Dad was. I should just come home. He added, "He is your father, you know."

I never understood why they felt I needed a reminder of our relationship. I know he's my dad, and I also know how he abandoned me after Janet's father accused me of taking advantage of his daughter. It was never me that needed reminding. It's him, and I've never heard anyone tell him: He's your son; you shouldn't kick him out.

But then hadn't been the time to get into all that, so I took the middle road like I always do. "Tell Mom I'll check back after work. I need to arrange to get some time off. Call me back if it gets worse." That was almost two weeks ago, and since he never called back, I just assumed everything was okay. Then Mom started calling on Wednesday.

I sat there wondering how, after so long, my mom would feel it necessary to consult me about a nursing home for Dad. I didn't know if I should be flattered that she cared about my opinion so much, or pissed because it seemed like such an obvious ploy to get to me. Since that was one of those problems I would never have an answer to, I decided to take a shower and call the house afterwards. I was drying off when the doorbell rang. I threw on my robe and ran downstairs.

It was Taylor Green and his son, Tommy. They had on matching Clippers sweat suits and Big Green's face was shiny with sweat.

"Morning there, sport," Big Green said. He grinned, glancing me up and down. "Whoa, getting a late start, I see."

"What do you want?" I said.

If he was put off by my rudeness, it didn't show. "Pamela called over a while ago and wanted to know if I had an extra Minnesota quarter for your son."

I stared at him in disbelief. Didn't this asshole have anything better to do than run around handing out quarters?

Little Green piped up, "I told Jackson he could-a had one of mine last week."

"*Could have* one, son," Big Green put his big hand on Tommy's shoulder.

Tommy corrected himself and continued, "Is he here? I gots it—have it—right here."

Big Green smiled. "The son and I were out jogging when the call came in. The wife said that Pamela sounded like it was important, so we brought it over as soon as we got back."

"It's a quarter," I told him. Then, but I don't know why, I explained to him what happened to the one I had last night. For some reason, he thought that was funny.

"You should put all your business expenses on a credit card, man. Then come tax time, it makes it that much easier. No searching the desk drawers for receipts." His eyes grew wide. "Hey! Why don't you let me set you up with my tax guy? We've been using him for years, and the man hasn't called yet."

Big Green was getting all excited about another way he could one-up me, like it wasn't enough that I had been a rotten dad for losing the Minnesota, but I was a lousy record keeper, too. I ignored the dad and looked down at Tommy.

"Jackson's not here. He and his mom won't be back until Sunday. Thanks for bringing the quarter, but I'm sure we'll run across another one soon." I made to close the door. "I'll tell Jackson you came by."

Taylor, Mr. Couldn't Catch A Hint If It Bit Him In The Ass, started to say something else, but the sound of the phone ringing cut him off. Thank God, I thought.

"That'll be my mom calling to give me an update on my dad's condition," I said right before shutting the door. I did feel bad about doing that to Tommy. He was a good kid. Probably adopted.

I grabbed the phone in the kitchen. It was Bobby, and he started the conversation with a sarcastic thank you for finally getting back to them.

"Don't you even care that mom has had enough to worry about without having to worry about you, too," he said.

"What's to worry about? There's nothing wrong with me." I could have added that if it was so serious, he should have called me on my cell phone. But I knew he didn't have my number either.

"Yeah, I know that, but Mom was beginning to think you were sick or something. That's the only reason you wouldn't call back, according to her."

"Well, I'm calling now," I said. "Just put her on the phone."

"She's talking to Mrs. Anderson."

"Who?"

"Dad's aide. You know, the woman you spoke to thirty minutes ago." I could see his big eyes rolling around in that big head of his.

Bobby was three years older than me, and we have always fought. Over everything and anything. Until I met Jeff and Jamal, I thought that was what all brothers did.

"Just let me speak to Mom," I said. He told me she was still talking to the aide, but I could hear her saying goodbye, and then the next thing I heard was Mom on the other end.

"John? Oh, thank goodness we finally got a hold of you." My mom sounded old. And manic. The sing-song lilt to her voice vanished, and her words were rushing out like someone was chasing them. In half a minute, she told me about Dad and how the doctors didn't think he was going to get any better, and filled me in on the nursing home discussions.

"That's what I—we—wanted to talk with you about, honey." There was a pause and a deep inhale. Then she continued, "I didn't want you to think we were going behind your back and making this big decision without you."

Her admission and the contriteness in her voice took me by surprise. I heard the low rasp of her breath moving in and out, but I didn't have a response for her. After I heard three exhales, she started again.

"We've been trying to reach you since Tuesday. Now here it is Friday, and I can't afford this at-home care much longer. It's not covered by the insurance. I remember telling your dad to get the extended policy, but he wouldn't. Said it was a waste of money." Deep breath. "Well, turns out I was right, not like that does me any good now. He can't understand anything we tell him now anyway." She was breathing normal now. "John? Are you still there?"

It was my turn to take a deep breath. "I'm still here; taking it all in."

"I know," she said. "So much has happened in the last two weeks." She paused. "It'll be nice to have my two sons near me."

I could hear Bobby in the background mouthing off about how I should have come two weeks ago when he called from the hospital. Mom ignored him, and so did I.

"Bobby and I have it narrowed down to two different places. Can you come this weekend and look at them and help us make the final decision?"

After I told her I would drive out later that day, she asked about Pamela and Jackson.

"They're in LA until Sunday. It's the anniversary of Grandma Rose's death. They like to act like she died two days ago." I tried to laugh, but Mom cut me off.

"I think it's admirable the way they respect their family—living and dead." Her voice became stiff, and since I didn't want our conversation to veer off into hostile territory, I told her to expect me in about three to four hours.

"I need to drop off some contracts at the office and make a few phone calls, and then I'll be on my way."

We mumbled our good byes, but before hanging up, I gave her my cell phone number. "You can call it if you need me," I said. After I hung up. I stared at the phone for a minute before heading upstairs to pack and finish dressing.

I was halfway up the stairs when I realized I had forgotten all about my scheme to get Mom talking about Janet and the Moores. When I reached the top, instead of going on to the bedroom, I turned around, sat on the top step and looked down the staircase. I replayed the conversation with my mom and decided that I would have to put Janet and all that old business to the side. At least for a day or two. I had no idea what I wanted to accomplish, but seeing her last night had been like getting tossed down a rabbit hole into an alternate reality that has been at the same time hidden and in plain sight for the last seventeen years.

When the downstairs clock chimed nine, I got up to finish dressing, stopping by the hall closet to grab the small suitcase. It was gone, so I settled on the next larger size. The set was a wedding gift from Pamela's old office. When my dad kicked me out of the house, they had stuffed my clothes into two big, black trash bags. Cheap ones that split open as I was carrying them up the drive to my aunt's house. I threw the designer bag on the bed and began tossing my stuff into it. Left with a Hefty, returning with Louis Vuitton. They probably wouldn't even notice.

Fifteen minutes later I pulled out of my driveway and headed towards the freeway that would take me to my office. I'm in the real estate business. Commercial only. Our company is connected with a contractor that builds those pod malls that pop up in the abandoned and depressed parts of cities. *They build 'em; we fill 'em*, which isn't as easy as it sounds. It's usually easy to snag a nail shop or doughnut hut and maybe a check cashing place, but beyond that, it's hustle, hustle, hustle. Mr. Matt Hudson, our boss, keeps a bulletin board up in the office that he has elevated to biblical status by calling it, The Board. One side lists the total number of empty spaces or pods we have, and the other side shows the dollar amount that we are losing each day. Whenever one of his disciples signs a contract, he announces that so-and-so has paid their contribution to The Board.

"And what have you done for The Board today?"

I've done plenty. That meeting I had last night—the legitimate one—was with the CEO of Lam Phuoc Foods, Inc. They own a chain of noodle shops in the northern Orange County area and are making plans to invade Los Angeles County with noodles, bean sprouts, and cilantro. He signed for three existing pods and promised to get two more that were still under construction. That should appease The Board, and Mr. Hudson, for a while.

I didn't start out in commercial. I used to be residential, selling overpriced ranch houses to newlyweds and young families too naïve to know any better. Couples would come in, charged up from watching some home remodeling show and describe, in detail, how they wanted granite counter tops, copper plumbing, huge windows, and about half a dozen other amenities they couldn't afford. My mentor told me that the first thing an agent needed to do was spend about a week talking clients back down to reality. I'm not what you'd call the patient type, so that was always the hardest part for me. I usually got along fine with the wives. It was the husbands that always seemed... distant. After about three weeks of working together, the husband would go to my broker and tell him that it just wasn't working out, and could they work with another agent. After that happened three times in a row, Kevin Duffy, my broker, pulled me aside and suggested that I think about the commercial side of the business.

"No husband-wife teams to bother with," he said. "Just you and the guys." Aunt Idell wanted me to come back to the appliance store. She said I made a mistake thinking I could sell fancy homes to white people. Kevin had mentioned nothing about that. He only said that the husbands probably found me a bit threatening. I didn't know what he meant until the wife of a client cornered me in the bedroom of a walk-through we were doing alone. She said she had picked up on my hints and wanted to know when I was going to make good on them. I let that one pass and signed up for a course on commercial real estate at the community college.

Kevin Duffy was the top real estate broker in the area. He had this god-like timing and never missed an opportunity. He always knew when to move forward or when to hold back. When to list or when to walk away. I met him while I was working for my aunt in her appliance store. After two years of being the stock and delivery boy, she finally put me out on the floor. She told me later it was the best decision she ever made.

"Boy, I don't know where you get that charm, not from your daddy, that's for sure, but you could sell ice to Eskimos.

She was right about both things. My dad had about as much charm as a Tasmanian Devil. He was a damn good plumber, but playing the salesmanship game just wasn't his thing. But for me, playing that game came easy, and I turned out to be a pretty good appliance salesman. Stoves, refrigerators, dishwashers, garbage disposals. All of it. I was too good, and when I wanted to move up to manager, she wouldn't let me. I meet Kevin Duffy and his wife when they came in looking for appliances for a kitchen remodel. Mrs. Duffy had dreams of having a high-end chef's kitchen, which Mr. Duffy knew was a waste of money and would price the house out of the market. "Talk her down," he whispered to me during their first visit. Aunt Idell was licking her lips over all that sales income, but I took the husband's side and steered Mrs. Duffy away from the over-priced stuff.

The whole affair took almost a month to complete, and during that time I got to know Kevin pretty well. I left the store right after he talked me into turning my stove-selling skills into selling homes.

The drive to the office took about half the regular amount of time due to the late hour and that Friday morning light all the traffic stations talk about. There was a community college and a high school within walking distance of the five-story office building. The building manager was forever trying to keep the outside grounds clean and free of over-sexed teenagers using the shrubbery as cover. When I turned into the parking lot, the grounds crew was out in full force. The sound of the leaf blowers drowned out my radio, and brown-skinned men dressed in jeans and dark green shirts hustled around the landscape pulling weeds, trimming hedges and whatever else those guys do.

One of the workers, the Black one, was a relative from Pamela's family, and had started working for California Grounds Keepers almost a year ago. Tyrone Sprey graduated from an average high school with a below average GPA and no idea what to do with himself, so it wasn't long before the street got a hold of him. After he came home with his pants hanging down around his butt and his new homies started hanging around the house, his family appealed to me to help him out with a job. The kid had no real skills as far as I could tell and when I asked him what he liked to do, he said he preferred working outside to being stuck in an office, so I introduced him to Jaime, the lead guy for this crew. I didn't really think that Tyrone would last, being the only brother on the crew and doing manual labor. But that kid surprised me and everybody else. Not only did he love the job, mowing lawns and all that stuff, he also took to working with people from south of the border like it was nothing. After his first year, he was semi-fluent in Spanish, had attended two quinceañeras, a dozen birthday parties, and he was dating Jaime's niece. His Uncle BJ blamed me for that last bit, but I couldn't see anything wrong with it. Tyrone was happy, staying out of trouble, and wearing his pants right again. Mr. Sprey said that they had hoped I would have turned him on to office work or real estate. I reminded him that his nephew was on probation for trying to sell a hot fax machine to an undercover and there was no way I was going to bring him into my office.

"Don't you trust him?" he asked me.

"No, I don't. Do you?"

Mr. Sprey didn't answer me, so Pamela added her two cents, "I'm sure his parents had higher aspirations for him than a gardener."

I said to both of them, "Hey, if the kid is cool with mowing lawns and working with Mexicans, so what? It's been almost a year and the police haven't been by once, Tyrone's calmed down, and I don't see him complaining."

No more was said about it after that, and to this day no one has thanked me. No one except Tyrone. I still think it was the interracial dating thing that bugged them the most. Tyrone could have shoveled shit for a living, but as long as he came home to a sister, the Sprey Clan would not have given a damn.

After I locked the car and was walking toward the side entrance, Tyrone waved me down. He caught me right before I went in.

"Hey man, a white chick was around here looking for you earlier." He was wearing the same uniform as the others except for the big straw hat. He had a black satin do-rag tied over his head that was so long it hung down the back of his neck, almost to his shoulders. He wore brown leather gloves and held the biggest rake I'd ever seen. He smelled like grass and gasoline.

"Looking for me?"

"Yeah. You. I didn't know her, but she knew who I was. Came right up to me and asked if you'd come in yet."

"What did you tell her?" I began seeing Kim around the same time I got Tyrone this job, so I had probably mentioned him to her at some point. I wasn't sure, but that's the only way she would have known who he was. She's not dumb enough to ask any stranger about me.

"I didn't tell her nothing, man." When I looked around the lot, he added, "She left about twenty minutes ago."

"Did she say what she wanted?" I asked, hoping he would say she needed some real estate information.

But he smiled. "You, man. She wanted you."

Okay, he knew. But that was all right. I did the cough thing. "She's just an old client trying to get out of her contract."

"She giving you a hard time about it?"

"Nothing I can't handle."

"Well, all right then."

No more was said because there was nothing left to say. He knew. And I knew he knew. And he knew I knew he knew. And it was as simple as that. No need for words of explanation or excuses, so I just patted him on the shoulder, told him to tell Lupe hi for me, and then I went inside, walked to the elevator, pushed the button and waited.

Two minutes later, I was walking into the office on the third floor. I had checked my phone on the ride up. There were three missed calls, all from Kim. I wondered what was so urgent. She had practically stormed out of the room last night, but that was nothing new. It only took me five seconds to decide to blow her off.

The office was up and running when I finally got there. I could tell by the look on everyone's faces that the weekly wrap-up/catch-up meeting was just about ready to begin. The wrap-up/catch-up, or WUCUs as they're called, was another of Matt Hudson's brilliant ideas. Every Friday, we meet around the conference table to either brag about how great our week was, or make up excuses to explain our underperformance. Mike was at his cubicle crunching numbers on a spreadsheet. He was very visual. Most of us preferred to bullshit with words. Lisa and Ted were rehearsing their excuses together, and Susie, the office secretary, was busy stocking the conference room with water and coffee. Susie was a small white woman just over five feet tall. Everyone in the office towered over her, making her look like a teenager rather than a twenty-five-year-old adult. She was a dropout from the college down the street who came into the office two years ago, and wooed Matt with her drive and focus. At the time, she claimed that she was only three classes away from graduation and had plans to go on to a university and major in business. Three months after he hired her, she moved in with her boyfriend and quit school to work full time to support him and his musical career. It didn't last, and when it finally ended, he left her with a couple thousand in credit card debt and an unwanted pregnancy. I heard that Lisa had helped with the baby situation, and then Matt gave her a little raise to help with the credit debt. Last week, I saw a half-finished college application on the computer screen. She's a good kid. I hope she makes it.

"He in yet?" I asked her as she breezed by me with a tray of sticky looking pastry.

"He called about ten minutes ago. Stuck on the 405." She disappeared into the conference room before I could tell her I was leaving. I looked around. Mike was up to his eyeballs in columns and numbers, so I bypassed him for Ted and Lisa. They worked together as a team and in past years that worked pretty well for them. Lisa would approach first, soften up the client, and then Ted would come in to close. But the old routine hadn't been bringing them in like before. I decided to give them my file to present at the WUCU. I didn't want to hang around to explain to Matt why I needed to leave, and I knew they would be relieved to present my good news in lieu of their own.

I explained my situation to them and handed the folder to Lisa, who grabbed it like a kid reaching for the last lollipop. Ted asked me how long I would be away.

"I really can't say. Mom wants to put him in a home, and I don't know how long that will take." I didn't want to be down there past Monday or Tuesday, but I couldn't tell them that.

Lisa, who was poring over my contracts, said, "That's really too bad, John. We lost Beth's dad last year." Her partner.

Ted grabbed the file from her. She started to protest but stopped when he said, "He didn't say his dad was dead. He said 'a stroke'."

She pouted and answered back, "It must be a serious one if they're putting him in a nursing home. Beth's dad refused to go to one, even though he would probably still be alive today if he had."

They were starting to get into it so I jumped in. "I said my mom was *thinking* about a home. No final decision has been made yet."

Lisa's eyes got big. "Maybe he can come stay at your place. With Pamela and Jackson. Beth and I considered that option with her dad."

Ted spoke up before I could say anything, which was good because I didn't have a proper answer for her, and there wasn't time to explain how the head of the KKK had a better chance of getting an invite to my house than my father had. It was not going to happen.

I waited, still not knowing what to say, but it didn't matter. Ted was chastising her for asking stupid questions, and Lisa was defending herself. Those two had the strangest male-female relationship I've ever known. Sometimes I just know he's banging her, but then at times like this, they act like brother and sister fighting over the last Pepsi in the fridge.

When they remembered I was there, Ted cleared his throat and asked me where home was. "You never talk much about it."

"Crown City, near Riverside. And up until now there wasn't much to talk about." Nothing I would want them to know about anyway.

Lisa frowned, "I thought you graduated from Washington High in Long Beach. Weren't you a year ahead of Beth?"

"I moved up here to live with my aunt when I was in the eleventh grade." I could tell she wanted to probe some more, so I cut her off with the old look-at-your-watch trick. It worked.

"You better get going," Ted said. "No telling what the 91 will be like this time of day. Lisa and I will take care of your WUCU report." We did the man-to-man eye gaze and then he added, "Don't worry about a thing." He meant both work and my family. I knew that, but Lisa didn't, and she couldn't resist that female urge to have the last word.

"I'm sure your dad will be okay, John." I tried not to laugh. Two minutes ago, she had him in the grave.

"He has to go, Lisa."

Thank you, Ted. We shook hands. I nodded toward Lisa and walked away.

"Call us with an update as soon as you know more," she said to my back.

I walked out of the office shaking my head. Lisa didn't give a damn about my father or me. She was upset over missing an opportunity to get into my business. Ted had understood that, too. Who says men don't know how to communicate? Sometimes less said is better.

Back outside, I looked around for Tyrone, but the crew had moved on. I had wanted to explain to him where I was headed and why. He was family after all. When I got to my car, there was a note stuck under the windshield wiper. I recognized the pink ink right away and contemplated not picking it up and letting the wind from the drive blow it away. Then it wouldn't be a lie when I told her I didn't get it. But this was so unlike her. She was usually more laid back than this. Coming around my job and leaving notes just didn't fit.

*I need to see you TODAY! Call me ASAP, K.*

I tore the note in half and shoved it in my pocket. I was about to get into the car when I thought I should dispose of it in a more permanent way. I didn't want to risk having Mom or Bobby see it. If she hadn't used that stupid pink ink, I could have claimed it was business or something. But serious business people aren't known for using pink ink. I stood by my car and had a mental debate about the best way to destroy the evidence when all of a sudden, I became so fucking tired and frustrated with all the lies, deceit, secrets, and cover-ups. I shoved the note back in my pocket, got in the car and slammed the door shut. If they should see it, I'd tell them it's none of their damn business and then ask them why they were going through my stuff. I started the car, backed out, drove toward the street and retraced my route back to the 605 freeway. There was a red mustang parked in the lot on the other side of the street. I drove right past it. When my phone rang, I ignored that, too.

Once I made the transition to the 91 freeway, the phone rang again. It was Pamela.

"Where are you? I called the office and Susie told me you left." Her voice was neutral, no emotion. I figured she was at her folks by now, and they were probably within hearing distance. I assumed she was still pissed about last night.

"I'm on the 91. I just headed out and was going to call you." I could have added, And where are you? But I didn't feel like getting into it with her. "I talked to my mom this morning, and she wants me down to help look at nursing homes for dad."

A little concern crept into her voice. "I knew it must have been a bad one. She kept calling all the time. You should have been down sooner than this." Pamela really liked my family and her defending my mom bugged me.

"I don't know how bad it is, and I'm going down now because I couldn't get away earlier."

I heard a heavy sigh. "Should Jackson and I come with you? Or, I could leave him up here with my parents and join you by myself."

The say no in her voice couldn't have been more obvious. And for that reason, I almost told her, Yeah, come on down! But I didn't. When I did finally tell her no, the relief in her voice was just as obvious. I asked about Jackson and told her to pay my respects to her parents.

"I will," she said. "Everyone understands why you can't be here."

Why wouldn't they understand? I was doing the same thing Mr. Sprey would have done if he were in my position. Does all his family value talk only apply to his family?

"Pamela, I wouldn't be going if Mom didn't need me—"

"I know that, John," she said. "But you know how you get down there. Just be sure you are helpful, okay?"

Even though she sounded like a mother warning her child to stay out of the principal's office, I let it pass. Mainly because she was right. My visits are almost always far from what anyone would call harmonious. But this time was going to be different. She should have understood that because she knew my father was in bad condition. It annoyed me that she would think I would cause trouble when my family was facing a tragedy.

"I know how to act, Pamela. You don't have to worry about me." If she caught the hurt in my voice, she ignored it.

"I'm not worried about you, John," she said. "Just be careful, okay?"

I forced out an okay, told her goodbye, then hung up. I was annoyed, but didn't want to dwell on it, so I tossed the phone on the passenger seat and thought about how differently my life would have turned out if Moore Drugs hadn't been the only place in town to get a condom.

# Chapter 4

Pamela Sprey taught at the real estate school Kevin recommended. She led the seminars on the ins and outs of escrow. Pamela had a Marilyn Monroe-type figure: big on top, a small waist and round on the bottom. The day we met, she was wearing a dark brown woman's suit with a white silk blouse underneath. The buttons were undone at the top, right at the point of remaining respectable. Women like her are good at knowing just how far they can go in their professional dress before it crosses that line, but whatever woman's magazine told them that was a good way to level the playing field was way off. Instead of us guys hanging around the water cooler discussing our female coworker's fashion sense, we usually spend our time imagining that top button popping open, or the skirt hiked up a few more inches. Someone should write an article about how it would probably be better if they stuck to turtlenecks and long skirts. Not that that would stop us from imagining.

The first night was a small class, about a dozen of us all hungry to start raking in those big commissions. Pamela began the class with one of those ice-breaker games where we each write two truths and one lie on a piece of paper. She would read each one and the others would have to guess who wrote it, and which statement was the lie. I wrote on my paper: 1) I graduated top of my high school class. 2) My aunt owns a successful appliance store. 3) Your tits are making me hot. The first one was the lie. When she got to mine, she read one and two fine, but stumbled when she got to the last one. She made up some excuse about not being able to read the writing and put it in her jacket pocket. After class, she asked me to stay behind, then informed me that she had used the process of elimination to figure out I had written that one. I didn't deny it. She asked if I'd had the seminar on sexual harassment yet.

"No. Do you teach that one, too?"

"No, I don't, but I strongly suggest you don't miss it."

I grinned and said, "Look, I'm sorry, but I didn't have anything else to write."

"I find that hard to believe, Mr. Roberts."

"John."

"I don't think it's a good idea for us to be so informal, Mr. Roberts."

She grabbed her briefcase from the table. "If I have any more trouble out of you, you'll have to transfer to another seminar."

I gave her my best salesman's smile and said, "I wasn't trying to cause any trouble, just having a little fun. If my note offended you, I apologize."

"Thank you, Mr. Roberts. I'll see you next week. Don't forget to do the readings."

"No, ma'am, I won't."

"Don't you want to know which one was the lie?" I asked right before she left the room. She hesitated, but said nothing and left me alone in the classroom.

I was a star student for the rest of that seminar. I did all my homework and was Johnny-on-the-spot with all the correct answers. On the last night of class, and after everyone left, I asked her out for a drink. To celebrate.

"This is just the beginning, Mr. Roberts. You still have a few more classes to take."

"John."

"John." She relaxed and rewarded me with a smile. I told her that for me, a boy who almost didn't make it through high school, this was something worth celebrating. She agreed, and that night over a glass of Chablis, she told me the story about her name and a little about her family and St. Paul. I mostly listened. I enjoyed seeing her in a relaxed atmosphere. She laughed at her own jokes and seemed to love and admire family. Especially her dad. I told her as little as I could about my background, but I did tell her about my aunt's stores, meeting Mr. Duffy and how he had talked me into switching careers. We talked about the real estate business and how it was finally starting to pick up again.

"You'll make a good salesman. You have that charisma about you," she said.

"You're the second person who's told me that."

"Well then, it must be true." She smiled again.

I tried not to beam like a stupid school kid. I wasn't use to getting compliments, so I mumbled a thank you and told her more about selling refrigerators. I think I sounded pretty stupid, but she didn't seem to mind. She asked a lot of questions and acted really interested in the answers. Then she leaned back in her chair and looked straight at me.

"So, your aunt does own appliance stores, and you didn't do well in high school."

"Are you using your 'process of elimination' again?" It was my turn to smile.

"You know I could have had you kicked out that first night."

"Why didn't you?"

"Let's just say I wanted to give a brother another chance."

"So how did I do?"

She leaned forward and rested her arms on the small table. "Fine, Mr. Roberts. You did just fine."

•          •          •

Traffic came to a crawl right before Yorba Linda, and after twenty minutes of stop-and-go, I pulled off. The drive to my parent's house typically takes a bit more than an hour, but it always seems like a lot longer. Probably because Crown City is in a different county and once you get out of Anaheim, the landscape completely changes. My hometown sits in a valley with the Chino Hills on the north and the Santa Ana Mountains on the south. Until the 90s, Crown City was just a town you drove past on your way to Riverside. But then housing developments started to pop up, bringing in wave after wave of families desperate for homes, but unwilling—or unable—to pay Los Angeles County prices. More people means more traffic, hence this Friday afternoon traffic jam and next to wishy-washy homebuyers, traffic jams tested my patience the most. I got out of dealing with home buyers by switching to commercial, and I hoped to avoid the stop-and-go traffic with a thirty-minute lunch and bathroom break. Mom and Bobby could wait; what's thirty minutes after a year?

I pulled into the first burger place I saw, parked and walked to the entrance; eating in my car was a big no-no. Nobody ate in my baby. Not even Jackson. A 2005 Lexus Sport Coupe is about as far as you can get from a traditional family car, but I deserved it—my reward for a successful sales quarter last year. I was bringing in the contracts like crazy, and everyone at the office was sweating their balls off trying to keep up with me. Even Lisa. Matt anointed me the Lucky One and awarded me a big-ass bonus. I took a couple hundred of it and treated Pamela to a dinner and theater night out in Los Angeles. The rest I used for the down payment. It was Matt who suggested the vanity plate: LKY JON.

Twenty minutes later, I was back on the highway. The traffic had lightened up, and before another hour passed, I was pulling off again, this time at the exit ramp to my parents' house. Corner lots that had been empty since my childhood now had gas stations, grocery stores, and other big-box chains on them. The people moving the real estate must have been making a killing since every time I come down some new shopping center or housing development is in the works.

I was so busy checking out the new landscape that I missed a turn, or took a wrong one. It was hard to tell. The only retail around here when I was growing up had been pumpkin patches in October and Christmas tree lots in December. Now every other corner had a mega-grocery or gigantic hardware store. I turned into a parking lot to backtrack and was shocked to find myself in the parking lot of Moore Drugs … and More. The name had changed, but I knew it was the same one Janet's family owned.

Jeff and Jamal's dad started Moore Drugs way back before any of us kids were born. It had been the first Black-owned business in the area, but it hadn't been here on this lot so close to the freeway. The Moore Drugs I grew up with was a much smaller store located a few miles from our houses. This one here was the brain child of Jamal, the twin with a head for business. Jeff had taken up the pharmaceutical side. The store in front of me was three times bigger, and under Jamal's guidance, had expanded its inventory to areas outside of prescriptions and over-the-counter drugs. That's where the *and More* part came in. In an effort to keep up with the competition, Jamal added small hardware and garden supplies to the inventory and had this new, bigger store built. Judging by the steady flow of people in and out of the front door, it looked like old Jamal had been right on the money with this scheme. It was just like him to know how to take an idea as strange as selling penicillin and potting soil and make it work.

I'm sure it took some fancy talking to get Jeff to go along. He was a more play-by-the-rules type of guy. He was always doing exactly what he was told to do, never straying outside the box, a regular Mr. Goody-Two-Shoes. Jamal had to threaten and bribe the hell out of him to keep him from telling the neighbors what really happened to Snowball. And all of those Lost Kitty posters hadn't helped, either. Every lamp post in the neighborhood had a poster on it begging for the return of that cat—daily reminders of our wickedness. After about a week we added vandalism to our rap sheet and started tearing them down when no one was looking. Next to Janet, I missed those guys the most. I parked my car and thought of an excuse to go in.

I was looking at get well cards, when he walked up to me. His arms were crossed, like a cop or something, and at first, I thought he was some jerk waiting for me to move. I glanced him over, annoyed, but when the recognition hit, I smiled. He didn't.

"Can I help you?"

Okay, so entering the store to get a card for Dad hadn't been the best idea. Did I want to run into one of the twins? Maybe. But the hostility? That surprised me. I never did anything to him, and I could never understand why the idea of me and his sister bugged him so much. And that hurt the most. I had considered them my best friends, and whenever we were together, it was always laughs and good times. We never fought—not the three of us together—but Jeff and Jamal would go at it sometimes. Everyone was amazed at how I had been the one to be their third wheel; the twins were so tight that it practically took a crowbar to break them apart. Mr. and Mrs. Moore used their influence to make sure they always had the same classes and schedule. And then all of a sudden, they allowed me, John Roberts, to join their duo. It was great, and I was eating dinner there two or three nights a week and staying over at least that often.

When I first started hanging out there, I hardly noticed Janet. She would dash in and out of the house like the Brown Hornet, off to this friend's house to swim, or that friend's house to go roller skating, or over to the park to play ball. Every once in a while she would pop back in so her mom could clean up a scraped knee or elbow and then not return until dinner time. The twins hated her in their room, so even when she was home I hardly saw her. Jamal teased her more than Jeff. He liked to call her the nappy-headed Tootsie Roll girl, and a bunch of other names meant to make fun of her undeveloped body. The one time I tried to join in, Jamal intervened and made sure I knew that that was not my place. He always acted like her protector. He was the one she would run to whenever she needed some kid from the neighborhood taken care of. Since I couldn't tease her like Jamal, and intimidating little kids wasn't my thing, the only communication I had with her consisted of playful arm punches.

And then Janet started to grow up. It was summer, and she had just turned fourteen. Her mom took her to New York for a family visit, and they were gone for almost three weeks. When she came back, that scrawny little caterpillar had magically transformed into a beautiful butterfly. My glances past her kept getting longer, and she was doing the same. Whenever we caught ourselves, she would smile like the Mona Lisa, and I would turn away tongue-tied. At first it was only harmless flirting. She was still in junior high, and high school guys going out with kids from junior high wasn't cool. So I held back and waited, keeping everything the same—going over for dinner, spending the night now and then, and using every ounce of energy to ignore Janet Moore. I was holding up pretty well, or so I thought.

One night in November I was over for dinner when she and her mom started talking about going shopping for a dress to wear to the upcoming Christmas Dance.

"They have dances in junior high?" I asked.

"Of course they do, don't you remember?" Jeff said in between bites of a fried pork chop. I looked at Janet. I was missing that smile—our smile—so I tried to tease one out of her.

"So, you got a hot date or something?" I asked, afraid of her answer.

Thankfully, she answered no and said that a bunch of her girlfriends were going as a group. That's when her father broke in.

"Janet's too young to have a boyfriend," he said. He was looking straight at me. "She knows it, and we enforce that rule. No exceptions."

I wasn't looking at him, but I could feel his eyes burning into the side of my face. Janet had lowered her head right after she rolled her eyeballs in a way that would have gotten her face slapped if her father had witnessed it. My heart thumped, and I took a gulp of purple Kool-Aid hoping someone would change the subject. After about a minute of silence, except for the clinking of forks on plates, Jamal nudged me in the shoulder, told me we were done, then asked his parents to be excused. Hanging out in their room, he was looking at me the same way his dad had when he started in about how his parents had big ideas for his little sister.

"They've already got her college picked out. It's in New York, way on the other side of the country."

"Who they plan on hiding her from?" I asked.

He shook his head and grabbed the exercise bar that went across the top of the doorframe and did a few quick pull-ups.

"They're hiding her from anybody who has the potential to get in the way of her plans."

"You mean their plans," I said, watching his biceps flex in and out.

He let go of the bar and dropped to the floor. "No difference, man. No difference."

"Don't you think it's a little late to get a card, man?" It was Jamal. He was standing right in the middle of the aisle, looking down on me. He wasn't smiling but there wasn't a trace of concern on his face either.

"Excuse me?" I said.

"Your dad has suffered a major stroke, he's paralyzed on the right side of body, his speech is gone, and he's fed through a tube. We don't carry any cards to cover all of that."

He was talking to me like I was a child, and he knew more about my father's condition than I did. I was pissed and surprised.

"My father is none of your business." I waved the get well card in front of him. "And what kinda business owner are you, anyway? How do you stay in the black when you seem to be intent on convincing customers against spending money in your store?" It was a pretty weak comeback, but it was the best I could do.

He stared me down with a quiet and deliberate concentration that scared the shit out of me. He was at least five inches taller, but I couldn't remember him being that big. My head came exactly to his chin.

"I talked to my sister last night, and I think it's a hell of a coincidence with both of us seeing you within a 24-hour period. Especially after almost twenty years of straight absence."

Jesus-Fucking-Christ, I thought. The phone lines between here and Long Beach must have been on fire with all the gossip and crap going back and forth. Now I was mad.

"I'm here to see my father, that's all. Seeing Janet last night? That was a coincidence. Seeing you today? That was a mistake." I turned to leave and threw the card I had been looking at on the floor. I stopped about ten feet from him to add, "And it won't happen again. I'll make sure to take care of all my pharmaceutical needs at the drug store across the street."

"Is that all you have to say to me, man?" he bent over to pick up the card. It had a picture of a beach scene with blue-white waves rolling onto light brown sand, dotted with sea shells. *May Our Lord Bless You with a Speedy Recovery*, was written across a clear blue sky.

"No," I answered him. "Fuck you."

# Chapter 5

I sat in my car and tried to calm the throbbing blood vessels in my neck. Matt had these anxiety attacks sometimes at the office, and it felt like it was happening to me. His attacks usually came after a terrible WUCU, which made sense; the man's entire life was tied up in that business. But trying to buy a card and breaking into a panic had not been in my plans. Jamal always intimidated the hell out of me, and I was mad that nothing had changed.

He hadn't thrown me out of the store, but it felt like it. Almost like when my dad threw me out of my house all those years ago. In the entire history of teenage romances, I know I wasn't the only teenage boy to get a girl pregnant. And it wasn't that big of a crisis. The only thing that went wrong was everybody's over the top reaction. If Janet and I had been allowed any say in the matter, things would have worked out better for everyone. I believed that then, and I stilled believed it that day as I sat in my car trying to halt a panic attack.

I looked around at the unfamiliar neighborhood and flirted with the idea of getting back on the freeway. I could go all the way to LA and be with my wife, son, and the rest of the Spreys. After I married Pamela, I tried to weave myself into the Sprey family tapestry. Since I considered myself a pseudo-orphan anyway, it seemed the natural thing to do. The question of which family to spend the major holidays with never came up. It was always at the Sprey's, with maybe a supplemental visit to my family home either before or after the big day. Jackson didn't mind; he said it was like having two Christmases.

It didn't take me long to talk myself out of escaping. Mom—and Pamela— would never forgive me. Besides, I already gave my excuses at work, and hooking up with Kim was about as appealing as a prostate exam.

I straightened up and re-evaluated my real purpose in coming back. Seeing Janet may have been the kick in the butt I needed to get me going, but now that I was here, it was time to get serious. And Jamal's description of my father's condition only underscored the situation. I pushed the Moores out of my head, started the car and left the parking lot of Moore Drugs … and More. What a stupid name.

After another wrong turn, I made it home. Bobby's old Dodge Ram was in the driveway behind Mom's dark blue Camry. The house hadn't changed—same Navajo White stucco with Saddle Brown trim, same St. Augustine green lawn, same evergreen shrubs, and Mom's small rose garden under the kitchen window. It was what we realtors call a starter home. Basic, solid, and no frills. Over the years the folks did the major upkeep—new roof, electrical upgrades, small kitchen remodel, and of course Dad kept the plumbing in tip-top shape. But they, along with the rest of the neighborhood, weren't big on the whole curb appeal thing so there would be no landscape architects, no fancy brick walkways or facades. Just having a safe and solid place to call their own was enough.

I left my bag in the trunk and walked up the path to the front door. It opened when I was halfway there, and my mother popped out of the house like a jack-in-the-box, bounded down the stairs, arms opened wide.

"You made it! I was just beginning to worry." I let her hug me close and the feel of her boney frame surprised me. Mom was always on the thin side, but not like this. She looked like she was starving, and not just for something to eat. She was wearing her standard polyester slacks and a pullover top. This one was dark blue with a mix of small multicolored flowers all over it. She's been wearing the same type of clothes for as long as I can remember. She told me once she stuck with them because they didn't need ironing. I had thought that was a silly reason to always wear the same thing, but Mom said she had enough to do without adding ironing to the list.

I pulled out of her arms and looked down into her face. At five feet, ten inches, I was the shorter brother, which means I am only three inches taller than my mom. Bobby takes after Dad and towers above me at six-two.

"I would have been here sooner," I said, "but as soon as I got off the freeway, I made a few wrong turns."

"Oh, honey, you should have called us or stopped for directions." She hooked her arm with mine and we walked into the house.

"Roberts Men don't ask for directions, Mom. Everybody knows that." Bobby had come in from the back room. We shook hands. I not only take after Mom in height but also in stature. Both of us are on the lean side while Bobby has Dad's bulky, muscular build.

"I have no problem asking for directions when I'm lost," I said. "Which I wasn't. One or two wrong turns doesn't mean you're lost."

"Okay, what does it mean, then?" My big brother chuckled.

"It means you made one or two wrong turns. That's all." This was an old, inside joke. Our father was famous for getting lost and equally famous for not asking for directions. One time, Mom tricked him into stopping at a gas station saying she needed a bathroom stop. Instead, she went up to the mechanic in one of the bays and asked him how to get to where we were going.

When she got back in the car she said, "You need to turn left here and then make another right on Manchester, which is three lights up." She folded her arms and stared straight ahead. I was about nine, and that was the first time I really saw my mom take a stand with him. She didn't say anything else the rest of the way, just used her fingers to point out turns to him. I felt proud to see her finally get her way with him.

Bobby smiled and I could tell he was thinking about Dad and how his driving days were probably over. His relationship with our father had always been more agreeable. By that I mean that Bobby had agreed to let Dad dominate and control and manipulate his life. Dad would make a suggestion, and Bobby would suddenly become enamored with the idea. Boy Scouts, football, track, going into the plumbing business, even his first marriage—all Dad's doing.

But that day he seemed scared, sad and lost all at the same time; probably wondering how he'd get on with his life now that his puppet master was no longer able to pull those strings. After a few seconds, he looked at me, reached out his hand, and spoke the nicest words he ever had: "Glad you're here, John. Mom and I could really use your help."

Okay, that threw me off. After the run-in with Jamal, I was primed and ready for a fight and had just assumed that Bobby would be my first victim. But the sincerity in his voice not only disarmed me, it left me completely speechless, so I just reached out to shake his hand again with Mom standing beside us beaming. She broke the silence by saying she agreed with her elder son.

"Now that my two boys are here, I feel much better." She gazed up at both of us, and I could tell she was on the verge of crying. I cleared my throat and took a step back. All that closeness was giving me a sudden case of claustrophobia. I turned towards the front door.

Mom's panicked voice stopped me. "What are you doing, John?"

Good question, I thought. Looking back at her teary eyes was more than I could handle, so I kept my gaze on the door and told her that I needed to get my bags from the car.

"I'll help," Bobby said, and before I knew what was happening, he was out the front door and making his way to my car.

When I finally caught up with him, he was fiddling with the trunk latch. "How do you open this thing up?"

I pressed the button on my key and the hood popped open. Bobby reached down to grab my suitcase and hauled it out. "Well aren't you Mr. Helpful today?" I said.

He straightened up and slammed the trunk door closed. Before I could protest, he let out a huge sigh. "This is gonna be a lot harder than I thought," he said, more to himself than me. He put my bag down and raised his hands up. On instinct, I flinched, but he just laid his hands on my shoulders and looked into my eyes.

"I promised Mom that I would do my best to get along with you." He came closer. "And I meant it. With Dad laid up like he is, and Mom having to make all these decisions, I thought it was the least I—we—could do for her. Okay?" Bobby didn't wait for my answer. He let go of my shoulder, picked up my suitcase and walked around me toward the house. I grabbed his arm to stop him.

"Look, man, I always come down here expecting to 'get along.' It's always been you and Dad who've started shit. Not me."

My older brother was silent for a few seconds. A neighbor drove by and did a honk-wave before turning into his driveway across the street. Bobby set my suitcase down again and said, "Well, since the only shitting Dad's doing right now is on a diaper, I guess you don't have to worry about that anymore." He went back into the house, leaving me with my designer bag and load of guilt alone on the sidewalk.

After about five deep breaths, I was ready to go back inside when my phone rang. It was Kim.

"Hello?" I said. I figured I had better answer it and get her out of the way.

"Jesus, John, where have you been? I've been trying to reach you all fucking day."

I could hear a long, raspy exhale and knew she was smoking, which meant something was wrong, so I asked her.

She started crying and all I could make out was words like, my fault, kill him and knocked up. That last bit caught my attention. I turned around and walked toward the street.

"What did you say? Put out that damn cigarette and calm down."

"Why do you think I'm smoking in the first place?" She took another drag. "Ever since I found out, it's been all I could do to calm me down."

The chain smoking wasn't working, but I didn't bother to tell her. Those words, knocked up, were sending me into a panic that no amount of deep breathing would be able to fix.

"Just slow down and tell me what's wrong." And then I asked, even though I really didn't want to know, "Who's knocked up?" It couldn't be her, and if she had told me it was, I'd know it to be some stupid trick she was playing on me. Probably still mad about last night. I had been making the usual overtures and hints that I was ready to end it, and I guessed she had picked up on that. Ending these affairs can be a delicate matter—say the wrong thing and it'll all blow up in your face. I went through that once before and was in no mood to go through it again. Besides, I don't think any husband can pull that off more than once and get away with it.

The scritch-scratch of a lighter and her raspy inhales told me she wasn't through trying to calm herself down. "Allison," she said. "Allison is pregnant by that asshole boyfriend she's been seeing this year."

I let go of the breath that I didn't know I had been holding. "Kim, why are you telling me this? What do you expect me to do?"

She blew her nose then answered. "I just needed someone to talk to, okay? Frank is in London, and he won't be back until next Friday."

"Did you call him?"

"No, I didn't. Telling someone their teenage daughter is pregnant is not something you can do over the phone. Besides, he'll just blame me, and I'm not ready to listen to his shit."

I needed to end this call and get back inside. Kim was on her way to telling me, again, about her non-loving, non-understanding husband, and I had exactly no time to listen to her.

"Look, Kim, I'm really sorry this is happening to you, but there's not much I can do about it. This is a family affair. Your family. When Frank comes back, the three of you can talk about it."

"But it's your fault," she hissed into the phone.

"Excuse me? I've never even seen that daughter of yours. My closet contact with her has been overhearing her screaming at you on the phone."

"I didn't mean you in that way, dumb-ass. I meant that it's both of our faults, yours and mine, for what we've been doing." She started to cry again. "I haven't been a good role model for her. She knows about us. I know she does."

"The only way she would know would be if you told her. Did you tell her?"

"No."

"Exactly. Look, Kim, I know you're trying to make sense of all this but blaming yourself isn't going to solve anything. And neither is blaming me. We are adults, okay? Allison is a child who made a stupid mistake. Hell, just take care of it, then get her on the pill and leave it at that. As her mom, that's really the best you can do."

"That's easy for you to say, John. You didn't see the accusing look she gave me when I found out. It was like she was saying, 'Well, what do you expect, Mom? You screw around too.'"

"And you're also a successful businesswoman. She could have copied that aspect of your life too you know, couldn't she?"

"Yeah … ."

"Exactly. She wasn't trying to be like you or follow your example; she was just being like every other horny teenager these days, and if Mother Teresa had had kids, they would have been screwing around too." I thought about how long I had been outside and knew it was time to get back in. When I looked at the house, I could see Bobby looking at me through the big picture window. I waved and pointed to the phone which seemed to satisfy him. He let the curtain drop and turned away.

"Kim, I really have to go. I'm sort of in a family emergency."

She sniffed into the phone. "That makes two of us. I didn't call to unload or get parenting advice from you, John. I called to tell you I can't see you anymore."

"Well … if that's what you want … if that's how you feel about it." This was going to be easier than I thought.

"I'm through with this, John. All of it. I've learned my lesson, and I just hope you learn yours before it's too late."

"I don't need to learn any lessons. I've known exactly what I've been doing all along. I don't kid myself about things."

"Really? Well all that self-confidence will come in handy when Jackson comes home to tell you about how his horniness got some girl in trouble. Goodbye, John."

She hung up before I could tell her how my son was none of her damn business, so I filed the memory of Kim away with the others. She still ended up being my last affair, but it wasn't because I was worried about Jackson growing up and impregnating teenage girls. I understood more than anyone how those things can just happen sometimes.

When I came back in the house, Bobby was sitting on the couch looking at some insurance forms.

"Where's Mom?" I asked, setting down my suitcase. I sat down in the chair opposite him.

"She's on the phone in the kitchen."

Before I could ask who she was talking to, she came in. "Oh, there you are, John. What took you so long?"

"Sorry about that. I was talking to Pamela. Things were getting a little emotional with Grandma Rose's memorial. She just needed to talk a bit."

Bobby opened his mouth to say something, but Mom raised her hand to stop him. She pinched her lips together and shook her head. Bobby let out a deep and loud sigh and went back to the insurance forms.

Mom closed her eyes for a second, like she was saying a quick prayer. When she opened them she said, "Your dad is awake now. Let's go see him."

I stood up. "Sure. That's why I'm here, right?" I didn't give much thought to their little exchange and just assumed it had something to do with the deal Bobby had made with her before I got there.

Walking down the hallway, Mom looked back at me and said, "I hope you gave Pamela my love for me. I really admire how they honor their loved ones."

"Yeah," I said. "Pamela's people are really big on family and tradition."

"And honesty," Bobby said. His laugh should have tipped me off.

We reached my parents' bedroom. When I was a kid, the walk to their room seemed to take an eternity, like a walk down a long, dark tunnel. The pictures on the wall were the same, only a bit faded. Mom had added pictures of her two grandchildren, each next to the son who was their dad. I gave mine and Jackson's picture a quick glance before entering the bedroom. My son looked just like his mother.

The first thing I noticed was that the old king-sized bed was gone, and in its place was a much smaller hospital bed. The mattress was raised at the head and the knees, making it peak and curve like a mountain range. My dad's massive body settled within the hills and valleys of the mattress like a rag doll that's had the stuffing beat out of him. He turned his head toward us, squinting his eyes to get a better look. They were blood-shot, and the lashes had specks of sleep-crust on them. Thin oxygen tubes rested below his nose and wrapped around his face, over his ears and disappeared under the sheets. He attempted a smile, or a grimace. His left arm curved into his body like a broken wing. It began to shake, but I didn't know if this was on purpose or just some spastic reaction he was having. Bobby and Mom moved toward him, but I stayed back, near the door.

"Look who has come to see you, honey." Mom's voice sounded like it does when she talks to Jackson—that sing-song, soft mothering tone. Mom turned to me.

"Come over here, John. Your dad is trying to wave to you." Now she sounded like a general shouting orders to her enlisted men. I took a few cautious steps towards the bed.

When it had all come out that Janet was pregnant, my dad had towered over me like an enraged black bear, ready to strike and tear into my flesh. If Mom hadn't held him back, he probably would have. I had never been more scared of another human being in my life. But that man was gone now, replaced by a quivering, drooling half-man whose every breath depended on machines, medicines, and my mother's care. God had transformed my bear of a father into a meek and helpless lamb, and I decided that He must be punishing him for past sins—that made sense to me. He had been a lousy husband, a horrible father, and this was his penance. But this is what I didn't understand: When I finally reached his bedside and looked down into those blood-shot eyes, I still saw that bear.

"Don't be afraid, Johnny." Mom put a reassuring hand on my arm. "He's still your dad. Go ahead. He won't bite you."

I moved closer, at a loss for what to do or say. Mom was talking, asking him if he knew who I was and telling him to say hi. Dad's eyes darted back and forth between the three of us towering over him. He looked confused and scared. His eyes widened when they finally settled on me. I took a step back.

Mom tightened her grip on my arm and urged me to say something. I opened my mouth, but nothing came out, so I ended up giving him a peck on the cheek. His face was warm and rough with beard stubble. Right after I straightened up from his side, he started hacking and convulsing. Mom darted around his bed and stuck some sort of suction tube into his mouth. It was just like the kind the dentist uses to suck up all that spit and blood. I could see Dad trying to raise his good arm to stop her, but someone had tied it to the bed frame. Bobby saw me looking at it and told me they had to restrain him because he kept pulling out his tubes.

"The old man's still putting up a fight," I said, but Bobby didn't answer back. He just stood there like a statue and stared at me with a look that made me feel defensive. Hell, I'd only been home half an hour and already the accusing had started. I let him fume and turned my attention to Mom.

"What happened to the nurse? The one that was here this morning?"

Mom had finished with the suctioning and was adjusting the oxygen tubes under his nose. "Mrs. Anderson? Oh, her shift ended about an hour ago." She tugged on the bed sheets to straighten them out. "She'll be back here in the morning. We can't afford twenty-four-hour care."

"What about a nursing home? Won't that be even more expensive?" I asked her.

"The insurance and Medicare will pay for a home, but not a full-time nurse at home," Bobby said. "Besides, Dad's too sick to stay here. You're seeing him on a good day."

"A nursing home was a hard decision to make, John," my mother said. "But your brother and I think it's the best thing to do. For everyone." Her voice was apologetic, like she thought I was blaming them or something. I wasn't.

"I know that, Mom. I was just worried about you. It's a big burden to take on."

She gave me a sort of half-smile and glanced at Bobby.

"We can't plan what happens to us, John. It just does, whether we're ready for it or not. And all we can do are the things that we think are right. That's all. Nothing more."

I took a reassuring step towards her. "I know that, Mom. I was just saying how I know it must be hard on you, that's all."

"She's not alone down here, you know," Bobby said. I could feel the tension starting to rise.

"I'm not blaming or criticizing anyone, okay?" I looked at my dad; he had fallen back asleep. "I guess I just hadn't realized how … ."

"We know, John." Mom interrupted me, patting my arm. "Seeing your father like this is a big shock. It was a shock to us, too. We've just had a little longer to get used to it."

She ended any further discussion by telling us to go wash-up for lunch. I did as I was told, not bothering to tell her I had already eaten. For some reason, I didn't think she could have handled that.

After a lunch of leftover meatloaf and potatoes, we finally got around to discussing the nursing homes they had picked out. I had eaten just enough so she wouldn't start asking questions like, was I all right or what was bothering me. I wasn't all right, and something was bothering me. But I didn't know why or what and wasn't in the mood to discuss me or my problems. That would come up later. It always did.

"The last one we looked at, Magnolia House, was the cleanest, but I didn't care too much for the staff." Mom said,

"It will have to be that one though, because they can take care of all the insurance papers and stuff." Bobby added.

I picked through the small stack of brochures and papers they had collected over the past week. Most of them had pictures of a smiling senior citizen in a wheelchair with an aide or nurse standing next to them, grinning down into their face with a look of loving concern. The old people in the photos all looked fine and that they could take care of themselves. There were no pictures of people who looked to be as bad off as Dad.

"Can these places handle someone in Dad's condition?" I asked them.

They looked at each other again, and I was beginning to feel like an outsider, or like someone who had come in late and missed the important parts. Which I had, but they didn't have to be so obvious about it. Mom got up to clear the table, and Bobby motioned for me to follow him outside. He led me into the back yard, turned to say something, but when he saw Mom through the window standing by the sink, he motioned me to follow him into the garage.

The garage was stuffed with thirty years of tools, garden equipment, and abandoned furniture. We had to pick our way around boxes, old lawn mowers, and power tools in order to reach the light cord that hung down from the ceiling in the middle of the garage. I looked around and saw two of my old bikes, a skateboard and some other discarded toys tucked away in a corner. Next to that was a Frigidaire freezer chest that Dad had bought during a deer hunting phase that lasted exactly one season.

He bought the freezer because, as he said, we're gonna need a place to store all that venison. Mom, of course, was against killing Bambi's parents, but Dad went anyway, and he took Bobby with him saying that I was too young to go. I had just turned ten and was beginning to understand the way of things around there, so I didn't really want to go. Mom and I spent the long weekend going out to eat and watching movies. We even went to the San Diego Zoo and spent the night at a hotel with a swimming pool.

When Dad and Bobby got back, the only venison he had was a 10-pound variety pack of free-range venison he had bought at a store on the ranch. Mom cooked some once, but then refused to ever again. She said that it stunk and made the whole house smell gamey. I never knew what happened to the rest of it, but the freezer stayed.

Bobby cleared his throat. "I wanted to get out of Mom's ear shot," he said. I knew that was what he was trying to do, and I suddenly became afraid of the reason he was doing it.

Bobby took a deep breath. It was uneven and his voice cracked when he spoke again.

"John, Dad is a lot worse off than you think, than we all thought. His condition will only get worse, not better. His doctor told us to 'prepare ourselves.'"

"Does Mom know?"

"Of course she knows, but she's doing what any wife would do, I suspect." I waited for more, still not getting his point. "She's pretending everything will be all right; that he's not so bad off."

"Pretending?" I said. "Well she's a pretty bad actress because she looks upset enough to me."

"Look, man, I didn't bring you out here to start an argument. We need to talk about what's going to happen—after." He shook his head.

I wanted to ask, after what? But I was pretty sure I knew what he meant. Instead, I asked him what he thought we should do … after.

"Well, they already have all the funeral arrangements and stuff taken care of. You remember cousin Ester from Ohio?"

"Yeah."

"When she was here about a year ago, she convinced Mom and Dad to take care of their arrangements before it got too late. Her husband had just died and she was full of these stories about fighting with the kids over every little detail. She was the first one of Mom's relatives Dad ever listened to because not too long after her visit, they sent all the paper work and forms to me."

"When was this?" I hadn't received anything.

He shrugged. "I don't know? Six, maybe seven months ago." He shook his head. "It's almost like he knew, ya know?"

I wanted to reach out to him, but my arm felt like it was welded to the side of my body. So I just told him how no one can really know these things. "They just happen."

That seemed to console him, so he went back to his reasons for secreting me away to the garage.

"So, what are we going to do about mom?"

"Mom? Is she sick too?"

"No, John." He looked really impatient with me, like I was teasing him or something, which I wasn't. I came out here to see about Dad, but I thought he was telling me that something was going on with my mom, too.

Bobby crossed his arms over his chest and looked down at me. I could tell he was serious.

"Mom's going to need taking care of after Dad's gone. We need to decide who's going to do what."

"Are you crazy, Bobby? Mom can take care of herself. Jesus, even I know that." He started to interrupt me, but I kept talking. "Hell, I always worried about her going first because Dad would be lost without her. Not Mom. No way."

"I don't mean take care of her like she's sick or something. I mean which one of us are going to look after her. Things like make sure she pays the bills, see that the lawn gets mowed, stuff like that."

Now it was my turn to get impatient. "Are we talking about the same woman? Because the Mom I know is probably in there, right now, making a list of all the things she's gonna do, and places she'll go once the old man is out of the way."

Bobby's fist smashing into the side of my jaw stopped me from saying anything else. I stumbled back, but didn't fall. The taste of blood filled my mouth, and for a few seconds the inside of the garage was a blur of black and grey with a few stars thrown in. Bobby was rubbing his hand and cursing—at me, or his hand. I wasn't sure.

"Shit, man. Why do you always have to be such an asshole?" he said.

I leaned against one of Dad's old sawhorses and rubbed my jaw. Bobby hadn't laid his hands on me since I was fifteen. I couldn't remember the reason, but I had probably deserved it. Teasing my older brother to the breaking point had been a specialty of mine. It was the only way I could get back at him for being Dad's favorite, but back then black eyes and bruises were easy to explain away.

"You need to fucking grow up, man," I said. "Look what you did to my face. I can't go around doing business looking like I was just in some gang fight or something." I spit a mouthful of blood onto the floor. "Shit. I think you knocked a tooth loose."

"You're lucky I only hit you once. You're talking about my father, you know. Not some stranger from the street." Bobby went to the freezer and stuck his hand inside. "I think I broke something."

"Serves you right," I answered walking over to him. "Give me some ice for my jaw."

He reached in with his good hand and pulled out a bag of frozen peas. "Here, use this."

I pressed the bag against my face and looked around for a place to sit. There weren't any chairs, so I walked over to the washing machine and lifted myself up. The dryer was next to it, with the door in between. Bobby used the dryer to sit down and pressed a bag of frozen carrots to his right hand. We were both quiet for a while, nursing our wounds. I spoke up a few minutes later.

"Whatever happened to all that deer meat you and Dad brought home that time." I hadn't been making a joke, so it surprised me when he started laughing.

"You never did find out what really happened, did you?"

I shook my head. "I just figured you guys didn't shoot anything. That's why he brought home the store bought stuff." Bobby hopped down from the dryer and went to put his frozen carrots away.

"Oh, he shot something all right. A buck. A big one, too. Trouble was, Dad got him right in the middle of his face. Looked like shit, man. Blood and brains everywhere."

"So what happened to it?"

"I don't know." Bobby walked back to the dryer and leaned against it.

"Why didn't you guys cut it up, or dress it, or whatever it's called, and bring it home?"

Bobby looked at me sideways. "Dad didn't want to."

"He didn't want to? You're kidding? After all the bragging he did and everything. What made him change his mind?" The peas were thawing, getting all mushy inside the bag.

"It was pretty gross, John. Like being in a horror movie, but for real. A dead animal with a million flies buzzing around. I guess it was too much."

"Too much for who?"

"For Dad. He threw up—a lot, and all over the place." He moved his hands in opposite circles over the garage floor to emphasize the perimeter of Dad's projectile vomiting. I tried to picture my father out in the woods, dressed up in his new camouflage hunting outfit, rifle in hand, bent over and puking his guts out over a dead buck with a blown out face.

"At first I thought he had caught some kinda virus or something. It took me a minute to figure out he was just grossed out."

"What did you do?"

"What could I do? It was as embarrassing as shit, man. The others were okay about it then, but I knew that they would be laughing their asses off as soon as we were out of earshot."

I hopped down from the dryer and threw the bag of peas in the trash. "So that explains why he never went back."

"That's a damn good enough reason if you ask me."

"Did he ever tell Mom?" I asked him.

"Couldn't say. She never said anything about it. I think she was just glad he gave it up." He looked at my jaw. "Are you gonna be okay?"

I rubbed my face, but it was numb from the ice.

"Yeah, man. I'm okay." Then I laughed. "You still got it in you, for an old man." He didn't join in my joke.

"Look John, I think it's about time we both grew up. Okay?"

I was quiet for a while, thinking about how two brothers, raised in the same house by the same people, could be so completely different. Grow up? That wasn't the problem. In my mind I was grown. Been grown since I got kicked out at sixteen. The problem was forgiveness, which I couldn't bring myself to do, even after nineteen years, and not because I'm stubborn or like holding grudges. It's because it's hard to forgive someone when they will not—or cannot—admit that they were wrong. Fingers pointed me out to be the bad one, and they have been quite happy to stick with that belief. I was probably pretty stubborn back then too, but hell, I was a kid. They were the grown-ups. They were the ones who should have been reasonable and protected me. My parents believed everything Janet's parents said, and every time I tried to open my mouth to explain, Dad's hand smacked it closed. He was judge and jury, and Mom just stood by and let it all happen. It all went down so fast, by the time I realized it was for real—really happening—it seemed too late to mount a defense. Aunt Idell had no problem welcoming me into her house. She said she had taken care of my father so taking care of me just came natural to her. She set up her spare room, enrolled me at Washington High, and put me to work in her store.

And now, after all of that, I am told to grow up, which was code for don't cause any more trouble. It was also the second warning that I had received.

But the worry on Bobby's face made me stop thinking about myself for a while. Despite everything, I couldn't deny the fact that he really cared and would probably miss Dad the most out of all of us. I wouldn't know how hard his death would hit me until … after.

"You don't have to worry about me. I know why I'm here." I said.

"Do you?"

"Yeah. I'm here to help my mother get things in order for Dad."

"Is that all? What about after that—?"

"Let's worry about 'after' later. Okay?"

Bobby wanted to say something else but stopped when he heard the screen door open and close. It was Mom.

"Bobby? John? What are you boys doing out here so long?" She opened the door. "What's wrong?"

Bobby spoke first. "Nothing, Mom. I was just getting John caught up on everything that's happened so far."

Her mouth twisted to the side in her *yeah right* expression. "Well if you're done, come back into the house. We have company."

"Who is it?" I asked when we were almost to the back porch.

She stopped and turned back to face me. We were out in the sunlight now, and Bobby's handy-work must have been pretty apparent because Mom's eyes zoomed in on my jaw, then over to Bobby. Through gritted teeth she said, "I don't need this right now."

Bobby started to say something, but I cut him off. "It's my fault, Mom. I was being stupid. Sorry, it won't happen again. I promise."

Her look of disbelief continued. After a few seconds, she said. "Well, come on inside." The three of us started moving toward the house again. When she reached the back porch, she looked at me over her shoulder. "I'll let you explain your face to Janet."

"Who?" I froze.

Mom climbed the two small porch steps and reached for the screen door. She glanced back at me over her shoulder and said, "Janet Moore. You saw her last night. Remember?" She walked through the door. Bobby stopped.

"What did Mom mean by 'last night?'" he asked me.

It came out as more of a threat rather than a question, but I freaked before I could give it any thought. I did not know why she was there, and I did not know why she had told Mom about our running into each other last night. All I knew was that I did not want her to see. "I can't go in there, man."

"What?"

"Janet's in there. Fuck, man. I can't let her see me like this."

Bobby let go of the screen door and it slammed shut. For the second time that day, he pulled me away from the house. "I can't believe you would be stupid enough to drag that family back into our business." He narrowed his eyes on me like Superman using his x-ray vision. "What the hell's the matter with you?"

I wrenched my arm from him. "I just saw her at the Denny's in Long Beach last night. She works there."

"And now she's here. What for?"

"I don't know 'what for.' I guess to see about Dad. She knew all about his stroke and stuff."

Bobby's face morphed into the same look of disbelief Mom's had earlier.

"Before last night I hadn't seen her in almost twenty years," I said. "Last night was just a freaky coincidence."

He began telling me how he didn't want any of the old shit to come up and, once again, to grow up. I just ignored him because time was passing, and I worried about her coming to look for us. I couldn't tell my brother why I didn't want to see her; I just knew I couldn't. I felt for my car keys in my pockets.

"Just tell them I had to go take care of some business or something."

I turned to leave by the back gate. Bobby shouted something, but I let his words fly right past me. He may have come after me, but I was on the other side of the gate jogging down the driveway to my car before I bothered to look back. He wasn't there. Then, like an idiot, I glanced up at the house and saw Janet sitting in the same chair I had been sitting in earlier, and my mom sitting on the couch. Mom was facing the big window, and when she saw me she jumped up like her butt was on fire. I gave a quick wave, pointed to my watch and mouthed: I'll-be-back-soon. Then I was gone. Speeding down Harkley Avenue away from what I had thought was my real reason for coming down in the first place.

# Chapter 6

I was at Jeff and Jamal's house that summer in 1986 when Mr. Moore brought Janet and her mother home from the airport. I remember him yelling at us to help with the luggage. We shut down the Atari and marched outside to the car in the driveway. I saw a woman standing next to the car, but her back was to the house. She had on a pale yellow sleeveless dress that hugged the curves of her body all the way down to right below her knees. She was looking at something on the other side of the car, and from behind she looked like Mrs. Moore. When I reached the car, she turned to me and said hi. I started to say welcome back Mrs. Moore, but when I saw the face, I realized my mistake; it was Janet, all grown up.

They had only been in New York for three weeks, so it wasn't like she had grown five inches or something. It was more of the way she dressed, the way she carried herself, and the total absence of that preadolescent awkwardness. She had developed a bit too. The last time I'd seen her she could have passed for a boy— flat chest and with dangly, skinny arms and legs that were always getting in her way. She was always tripping or falling down, and her legs and arms would be forever covered in band aids and smelling like Mercurochrome. But looking her over in that dress, all I could see was her smooth brown skin and I knew I was staring, but I couldn't help myself. Plus, she didn't seem to mind, so I kept on. I examined her dress and discovered that it wasn't really yellow. It was white with about a million tiny yellow flowers over it. My eyes drifted to her chest where I saw an array of yellow daisies stretching across two round bulges. At first I thought she must have stuffed her bra because there was no way she could have grown those in just three weeks. Later, I discovered how good she had been at covering herself up with oversize T-shirts and baggy clothes. While I stood there staring at her, the twins had made their second trip out to the car and taken in the last of the suitcases. Jamal yelled something at me from the porch that brought me out of my trance. Before I could ask him to repeat what he had said, he disappeared into the house. I glanced around and realized I was alone with Janet. I looked back at her and couldn't think of one god-damned thing to say. Then she laughed,

"Hello, John. Don't you recognize me?"

I answered her, babbling like an idiot, "No. Yes. I mean—Janet?"

She laughed again, "Yeah, it's me. Who else could it be?"

"I know it's you," I said. "You just look … different." By her reaction, I knew I had said something wrong. The smile dropped from her face, and she glared up at me.

"Yes. I look 'different.' That's all anybody's been saying: 'Oh, Janet, look at you. You're all grown up!'" She took a step back and away from me. "I've been home three hours and already I'm tired of hearing that."

I knew right then that something had happened to her, but I was too young to understand what. I tried to get the old Janet back by punching her in the arm like I use to, but she was too quick and I missed. Then she bent to pick up her small bag and walked away saying, "You're so immature, John."

I ran after her not knowing what I wanted to say, but knowing that I had to say something to make everything all right. We reached the front door at the same time, but her dad was standing in the doorway. He glanced over his daughter and then let her pass through. He gave me the same glance, and I stood there feeling like I had done something wrong. Finally he said, "John, the family wants to spend some time getting reacquainted."

He had said family, which did not include me, but I didn't realize he was trying to get me to leave until he held his arm across the doorway blocking my entrance. "Alone," he said after he realized that I was slow in getting his drift.

When it finally sunk in, I was more hurt than embarrassed. I turned away and headed down the street. Mr. Moore had asked, or told, me more than once before to leave his house, but this time it hurt. I couldn't help but think that I would be missing something important. I imagined Janet and her mom sitting in the living room, the others sitting around listening with fixed attention to all their New York adventures.

A dark cloud of pity formed over me as I walked home. I stood in my living room and waited for someone to notice the state I was in, but all eyes were glued to the TV. After a few minutes, I turned away and went to my room. A good door slam would have been a little comforting, but Dad took it down after I had slammed it one time too many.

After school started in September, things returned to normal. Everyone got used to the new Janet, and the comments and stares stopped. The twins and I got back to our old routine of hanging out. Janet began the ninth grade at the junior high school, and the twins and I started our junior year at the high school that Janet would attend the following year. Ever since she'd called me immature, I had been keeping my distance. Her brothers, who used to tease and arm wrestle her, stopped. Jeff confided in me that their mom and dad had warned them to stop teasing her and to treat her like a lady. He said his mom told them how Janet was having a hard time growing up without a sister or best friend to talk with.

"I told them that it wasn't my fault she didn't have any girlfriends. She's been running around acting like a boy all this time, what did she expect?" Jeff said.

Things were changing in the Moore house, and the biggest most noticeable changes were coming from Janet. All the time she used to spend outside running around like a savage, she now spent inside either on the phone or flipping through a copy of *Essence* or *Jet Magazine*. She spent a lot of time in the bathroom too—doing what we never could figure out. The twins didn't seem to give her change much thought. Jeff's teasing centered around the boys he heard she was talking to, even though we all knew she wasn't because of her dad. Jamal let all potential suitors know that his sister was off limits. I was with him one time when he thought he saw Eric Baker making a move on her. Jamal put his arm around Eric's shoulders, real smooth like, and started doing his Marlon Brando-Godfather impersonation:

"You messa with my sista, you messa with me. Capisce?" I thought he was pretty funny. He did a pretty good Dirty Harry too, but Jamal had a round, chubby face that fit the Brando routine much better.

So, that was how it went for about three months. Janet growing into her adolescence. Jeff trying his hardest to treat her like a lady. Jamal, her unofficial bodyguard. And then me in the middle of it all, trying to hold on to my precious place in their good graces. At the same time, I was holding back the tidal wave of emotions that would swell up in my chest every time I caught myself looking at her. Now I knew why they called it a crush. It's because you feel like all your vital organs will collapse under the weight of all that emotion.

Finally, in a desperate act of self-preservation, I cut back on my visits to their house. I wanted to believe that I would have been exempt from Jamal's bullying form of brotherly protection. After all, I was supposed to be one of his best friends. And who better to date your own sister than your best friend? If I had a sister, it wouldn't have bothered me. But I didn't have a sister, just an older brother I couldn't even talk to, so I ended up spending more time at home. Dad had put my door back up when school started, so at least I had that.

Right after Christmas break, Jeff called and asked me to come over. It was Friday night and he said that everyone else would be out.

"Janet's going to that dance, and Jamal is going out with Brenda. Again."

Brenda was Jamal's on-again-off-again girlfriend. Jeff didn't like her too much, and neither did the rest of the family. I don't really think Jamal cared for her too much either, she was just his standby girl as he liked to call her. I had nothing better to do, so I told Jeff, sure. Besides, I was beginning to miss being with them. As I walked down the street to their house, I kept telling myself that I was going there to hang out with Jeff, nothing else. We planned to watch some kung fu movies and maybe play a little one-on-one in the driveway. Janet wouldn't be there anyway, so I could at least relax and not worry about running into her and doing (or saying) something stupid. By then, my feelings for her had grown so out of control that I felt like a blubbering idiot every time we were together. So I did what any teenage boy would have done. I ran away. But that night was going to be different. She wouldn't be there, and it would be just Jeff and me hanging out like old times.

When I reached their front door, I debated whether to knock. I had stopped knocking early last summer because Mrs. Moore kept telling me to just come on it. But I hadn't been over in a month, so I wondered if my just come on in pass had expired. I had just made up my mind to knock when the door opened.

Of course it was her, standing there all dressed up, and of course there I was with my fist raised right at the level of her face, looking like I was getting ready to punch her in the mouth. My timing couldn't have been more perfect.

We each took a step back. I fell from the step and landed on my ass in the walkway. Janet tripped on the hem of her gown, tearing a hole about two inches from the bottom. I heard her curse—at the damage or at me, I couldn't tell—and then her parents were at the door asking what happened. I scrambled to my feet, opened my mouth and felt about a million apologies spill out, just like a blubbering idiot. By the time everyone had calmed down Janet was off to her mother's room so she could fix her dress, and Jeff had hustled me into his room past the glaring eyes of his father.

"Shit, man. What did you do?" Jeff asked as he closed the bedroom door. He was laughing, and I wished I could join in, but I was still way too embarrassed to find anything funny.

"I didn't do anything. She just scared me when she opened the door so fast, that's all."

"Janet scared you?" He sat down on his bed, the bottom bunk. He was still laughing at me.

"Not scared, man. You know, I was just surprised to see her, that's all." I used their old weight bench to sit down. The weights were stacked in a corner, underneath a few holes in the wall Jamal had made whenever he tossed, instead of placed, the weights back to their stack. I stared at the holes.

"You said that everyone would be gone." I was accusing him, but I really needed to make it not my fault. Backlash from Jeff didn't worry me, but if Jamal had been there, I would have wobbled home ten minutes later, nursing my wounds. And that wasn't the only difference between them.

Besides being completely different in body structure—both were tall but Jeff was tall like a basketball player, Jamal like a defensive lineman—they were also complete opposites when it came to the social aspects of their lives. Jeff liked to enter a room, find a corner somewhere and just hang back until he had surveyed the room and everybody in it. Jamal entered like a bull and let everyone know he was there. And everybody would always know that Jamal had been there, but with Jeff people would ask, "Was your brother there? I can't remember. Where was he?" Even though the people never remembered him, Jeff not only remembered who was there, he also made mental notes of who wasn't. It was creepy, like he was memorizing everything just in case he had to give a detailed description to the cops or something. And that's exactly what he had been doing that night as I sat there staring at those holes in the wall—studying me and making mental notes for later. About half a minute later, he must have registered and stored all the info he needed because he got up and started setting the VCR to play one of his old kung fu movies. Bruce Lee was his favorite. After the movie started, we both heard the front door open and close, and then the house was completely quiet.

He paused the tape and said, "Want something to eat, man? I'm starving."

We spent the rest of the night doing what we had planned: more kung fu, Bruce Lee ass-kicking, eating everything from cold hot dogs to some stale peanut butter cookies we found in the back of the pantry.

It was almost ten when I began to wonder (worry) about what time his folks (and Janet) would be home. But I didn't want to ask him. For the last three hours, we had been talking about everything but that and I wanted to keep it that way. I figured Janet's curfew was probably ten, maybe ten-thirty at the latest. I couldn't imagine her dad letting her stay out longer than that. I checked my watch. It was exactly ten o'clock. Jeff had been observing me.

"You gotta go?" he said.

I should have said yes and left right then, but I didn't. The only excuse I have is that my ignorance and raging hormones had taken over both my body and my common sense. Jeff kept looking me over, so I excused myself to the bathroom.

After I finished, I stepped out and found myself right in front of her bedroom. The door was open, and I could see some of her clothes scattered across the bed. Her room still reflected her Tom-boy days: a plain twin bed pushed up against the wall, covered with a burgundy bedspread. The other furniture was just as plain; a chest of drawers made of some dark colored wood, and a small desk that sat under the window. One thing that hinted it was a girl's room was the white vanity table next to the bed. It had pale pink lacy fabric around the sides that hung down around it like a curtain. The same fabric was on the stool. The top was bright white, all shiny and new. I figured this piece of furniture was the first phase of the redecorating plan. There were other girlish signs too: a Michael Jackson Thriller poster tacked to the wall along with Earth, Wind and Fire and Chaka Khan. At the head of her bed there was a pile of stuffed animals. The taller ones, a giraffe, a few bears, and a big yellow monkey, were laid out in a semi-circle around ten or fifteen smaller ones. Right in the middle of all that, she had placed a medium-sized brown dog. It had huge ears that hung all the way down to its paws. Its mouth was open and a little pink tongue poked out like it was waiting to lick someone. It even had a pretend dog collar around its neck. Cute. I walked over to get a closer look, and imagined her in her nightgown, replacing each animal in its specific spot every morning after making her bed. When I got closer, I noticed the tag on the collar. It was turned backwards. Without knowing what I was doing, I picked up the dog and turned the tag over. A label on it said: Hi! My name is: below that, she wrote J.R. in red ink, and drew a heart around it. I smiled so big I thought my face would crack.

I put the dog back, making sure it was in the same position, and took a few steps away from the bed. I know my mind must have been racing with hundreds of thoughts and ideas and possibilities, but I can't remember what they were. All

I do remember is feeling a wonderful sense of relief at knowing that I had not been wrong about her and how she felt about me. That alone made me happy, knowing that I wasn't delusional or going insane. And just the possibility of us being boyfriend and girlfriend made me happier than I had been in weeks. I didn't even contemplate that J.R. could stand for anybody else. It had to be me.

The only other thing I remembered doing was wondering how I could leave her a note or figure out some other way to get a message to her. I was looking over at her desk when he walked by. I turned around and he was looking right at me. I looked back at the stuffed dog, not remembering if I had turned the tag backwards again. I hadn't. When I looked back at Jeff, he was shaking his head back and forth at me like I had just got caught with my hands in the cookie jar, which I had, so I waited for him to tell me off and kick me out of the house. But he didn't.

He only shook his head and said, "Forget about it, man. It ain't gonna happen."

I started to ask him what he meant, but I sensed that he wasn't in the mood for playing games. So instead I asked him, "Why not?"

Before he could answer, a car pulled up into the driveway. It was his parents. Jeff nodded his head towards the sound and said, "That's why, man. Even you should know that." He turned to leave and I followed him, right after I turned the dog tag around.

At the end of the hallway Jeff told me that I better get going. I didn't even think about arguing with him. I left through the back door, and Jeff walked with me outside. I wanted to talk with him, but I held back. Jeff was a man of few words and he was nearing his limit. He walked with me out to the sidewalk then he asked me what Bobby had been doing tonight.

"I don't know. I guess he went out with Moon," I said.

"Moondera Wilson?"

"Yeah, that same girl he's been dating ever since junior high."

He let out a soft whistle and called her a foxy lady.

I couldn't agree with him. Moondera did have a fine body, but her big mouth and sassy ways overshadowed any of her other qualities. She was too much like her momma; always threatening to cut someone or mess 'um up good if they even looked at her wrong.

"That's the kinda chick you should be going after, man." Jeff said. "Why don't you get Bobby to set you up with her sister or cousin or something?"

"Why? So I'll be out of the way?"

Jeff put his hand on my shoulder and said, "Look, man, I'm just trying to look after you, that's all." He pointed back to his house, to Janet's bedroom window. "Cause ain't nothing gonna happen here. My folks have already decided that."

"Isn't that her decision?"

Jeff laughed. "No difference, man. No difference."

# Chapter 7

I was away from my parents' house for over an hour. I kept driving but had no clear destination in mind. I should have stayed at the house, and I was mad at myself for running away like I was being chased by cannibals. Janet couldn't have come to see me. She didn't even know I was home, and it wasn't like she, or any of them, ever dropped by to be neighborly or something. Back when we were kids, I was always at their house, never the other way around. Bobby had accused me of being too ashamed to invite them over. But that wasn't it. I just wanted them for myself. He had Dad after all.

I turned back onto the same street I had gotten lost on earlier and found myself driving past the drugstore when it hit me. Jamal must have told her about seeing me in the store. I zoomed past, realizing that this visit was going to be no different from before. Back then, I couldn't even take a shit without everyone knowing how many sheets of toilet paper I used.

After about 20 minutes of mindless driving, I turned into the parking lot of the first Kinkos I saw. We have some business down here, but not much. I figured that as long as I was down, it wouldn't hurt to look into a few sites. Also a good way to kill some time. I called Susie and asked her to fax me the addresses and contact info on a few clients. She tried to give me a hard time for working when I was supposed to be taking care of my dad. Everyone telling me what to do was getting to me, so I mumbled an excuse, hung up before I heard her response, and waited for the faxes to come through.

The addresses were all on major streets, and it didn't take long to locate them. The last one was about seventy-five percent complete, but it also looked like most of the pods were taken. There were *Coming Soon!* banners on almost every store front. I took a few pictures, and drove back to the Kinkos to fax some info to the folks at Lam Phuoc, pretending that they may be interested.

After that, I figured enough time had passed, so I started back to the house. My face had stopped throbbing, and the bruising wasn't as bad as I thought it would be.

When I made it home, it was close to dinner time. The only other car near the house was my mom's. I wondered how long Janet had stayed, but I wasn't going to ask. Bobby would be back to help turn Dad over and do whatever else needed doing for the night. That was good because I wasn't going to do any of that stuff—lifting him, or suctioning up spit, or wiping his ass.

Mom was busy in the kitchen, so I yelled that I was back, threw the faxes on the coffee table and headed to my old bedroom. It's a three bedroom house. My bedroom was on the same side and next to my parents' room. Bobby's room was on the other side of the house, next to the kitchen. Bobby had the room farthest away from them; a distance that allowed him to get away with staying up late and all kinds of other shit he'd do in his room after Mom and Dad turned in. My proximity meant that even keeping the light on passed bedtime didn't go unnoticed. But there were benefits. One night I was having a coughing fit and the next thing I know, Mom is standing over me with a spoonful of cough syrup in my face. They heard everything.

My suitcase was waiting for me on my old bed. My room was now called the guest room, not that they had frequent guests, but calling it the guest room is a lot easier than saying John's old room. Bobby's room was now the craft room. Mom had taken up all sorts of crafts and sewing projects. She sends us things like embroidered pictures, decorated frames, painted statuary, crocheted doilies, and other little projects that Pamela always found a place for in the house. It would sit there for months before I noticed.

"It's been there for a while," she would answer when I finally said something about whatever it was. The quality improved over time, and I remember Pamela telling Mom that she should make a business out of it, but Mom dismissed the idea as being silly. I decided to bring it up later since keeping busy is one of the best ways to handle that time ... after.

I finished unpacking and walked back down the hallway. Mom was in the kitchen standing in front of the stove stirring a big pot. The smells that filled the room brought back a few childhood memories. Good ones.

"Are those ranch beans, Mom?" Ranch beans were my favorite dish—the way she cooked them, and she always made them for me whenever I came to visit. But I hadn't expected her to take the time to make them now. "Mom, you shouldn't be messing with that now, not with all the other stuff you have to do." I got a soda out of the refrigerator and sat down at the kitchen table.

She adjusted the flame, covered the pot and sat down opposite me in front of a glass of watered down iced tea.

"What trouble is a pot of beans?" She took a sip before continuing. "I wish everything else was going to be as easy as cooking beans."

We were both quiet for a while; Mom rolling the glass between her small hands and me sitting there waiting because faking it with Mom never worked. And now wasn't the time to try to bullshit her. So, not wanting to talk about my quick exit, I asked about Bobby. She took a deep breath that lifted her shoulders up and down. I could see her collar bones jutting out on both sides. She picked at her lunch, and I wondered how she must have been picking at all her meals the same way.

"I've wanted to talk with you about him, honey. I'm worried about him." She said.

"Bobby?"

She lowered her eyes. "I don't think he really understands how serious this is."

"What do you mean?"

When she looked up, the worry and sadness in her eyes made me uncomfortable. I tried to focus on the pot of beans.

"This isn't your dad's first stroke, John. He had a mild one about six months ago."

That bit of information made me look straight back at her.

"A stroke? Did you tell me about that one because I—"

"We didn't tell anyone because it was such a small one, wouldn't have even known about it if he hadn't been going to the doctor for those constant headaches. They ran some tests and told us he had something called a TIA. Besides the headaches and a little bit of confusion he had, there wasn't that much else wrong, so we decided not to tell you."

"Or Bobby? Does he know?"

"No, he doesn't, and that's what I want to ask you."

"What?"

Mom looked at me the same way Bobby had in the garage. She talked, and I listened. She wanted me to not tell him how serious Dad's condition was. She was worried how he'd cope after, and who was going to see that he was taken care of. It was weird the way they both used the same language, and I just sat there half listening since I had heard it all before. They wouldn't have had the same conversation about me since both of them only worried about each other, not me. I guess they assumed that I, out of all of them, had the least at stake. Were they right? I couldn't answer that, but I do remember thinking how it would have been nice to have Pamela with me. With her, I had a better chance of at least one person worried about my feelings.

When she finished talking, I took a big swallow of soda, and told her that, no I wouldn't tell Bobby how bad off Dad was and yes, I'd try to be supportive of him after. I finished the Coke and squeezed the can between my hands. The aluminum gave way underneath my grip, and with that little act of destruction, something started to stir in me. I squeezed it harder until it was almost flat in the middle, then I folded it in half, laid it on the table and flattened it some more with the palm of my hand. When I finished, I looked around for other things I could crush and destroy. Mom was watching me with that look on her face, still worried about her precious Bobby.

I stood up and threw the flattened can into the trash.

"Got any beer?" I asked, going back to the refrigerator.

"There should be one or two in there somewhere."

There was one left, and I grabbed it. We both sat. She played with her iced tea; I swigged down my beer. Mom broke the silence by asking me about the business I'd had to take care of earlier.

I took a deep breath. "It really wasn't anything that couldn't have waited. I just needed to get away. That's all."

She dropped her chin down and looked at me over her glasses. I didn't have to explain from whom I wanted to get away.

"That was a long time ago, John."

"Was it? Because all of a sudden, it seems like it happened yesterday." I stood up and paced around the kitchen, something I did when I felt agitated. My father had the same habit. "The thing is Mom, this whole business with Janet and me and her family and Dad never got made right, you know. I thought I was past all of it, but when I saw her last night, it all came back."

"What came back? You were just a kid, John."

"I still know what I felt, Mom. So did Janet."

"That was a long time ago. Now you have a wife who loves you and a son who needs you. You can't afford to be going back to fix things or make them right." She stood up and stepped to the sink to wash her glass.

I knew right then wasn't a good time for this conversation, but something inside urged me forward. I felt like I was running out of time, or that the time had finally come. Later, I would realize that my new found courage came from the belief that my major detractors were out of the way. Mr. Moore had run off to some tropical island with his new young wife, and my dad could barely breathe on his own, let alone stop me from setting the record straight. Besides, according to Mom and Bobby I didn't care about him anyway, so then seemed as good a time as any.

"I may have been a kid, but I'm an adult now."

She turned around. "So what John? Are you going to leave your wife and son to be with her? Is that what you want? Is that what an adult would do?"

"No."

"So what's the point in bringing up all this old mess?" She waved an accusing finger at me. "You have a lot more to lose this time, and just trust me when I say it wouldn't be worth it."

"The only thing I have to lose is the shroud of guilt everyone forced me to wear all this time. We didn't do—"

Mom's voice was loud and on the verge of hysteria when she cut me off.

"They were going to accuse you of rape, John. Rape. What were we supposed to do? Her father could have taken it to the police and who do you think they were gonna side with? Who?"

I didn't answer. It was the same old argument that they always gave; sending me to my aunt's was a lot better than letting me go to juvie. But the rape angle was just some bullshit her dad had made up. Janet wouldn't have told him that. Her parents had come over, told my folks that Janet was pregnant, and I was the father. When my dad asked what they were going to do, Mr. Moore looked at me like I was a bug he wanted to stomp on. "He had to have forced her," he said. "My Janet would never consent to anything like this with him. Never."

I had been sitting in the corner, listening. I just sat there quiet, like a stupid asshole, waiting for my parents to turn around and ask me what really happened. But right after Mr. Moore spoke, my dad jumped on me, and I knew I was going to die right there in my family's living room. He was yelling at me and I could hear Mom crying in the background, telling him to calm down. He hit me across the face so hard that I fell over and smashed into the china cabinet. I could feel glass and wood splinters cutting into my face and arms. He started grabbing me by the collar when Mr. Moore came from behind and held him back. He was telling my dad to take it easy and that he and his wife had planned on keeping it in the family.

"We don't want this spread about town Walter, and we know you feel the same way."

My dad wrenched his arm away, but he was breathing too hard to say anything. Mom had come to my side by then, checking the cuts on my face and arms.

"I think he's going to need stitches, Walter."

My dad was silent, still trying to catch his breath, but Mr. Moore panicked. A hospital visit would blow his keep it in the family plan.

"Look," he said, "I can get bandages and stuff from my pharmacy. I'll even get him some pain killers and antibiotics if he needs them." He looked straight at my father. "We don't need to make a bigger mess out of this than it already is, Walter. Okay? Let's all just calm down for a minute and think about the best way to handle it."

Mom shuffled me into my bedroom while the rest of them sat back down to talk. She forced me to wait while she collected the first-aid kit from the bathroom. Mom was trying to clean me up, but I kept telling her I wanted to go back in the living room and tell them what had really happened. She wouldn't let me, and kept on saying how I had done enough, and it was out of my hands now.

"But what about Janet? I need to see her."

She stopped her first-aid to my face and grabbed me by the shoulders. Her eyes narrowed on me, hard and fast.

"You put that girl out of your mind right now, John B. Roberts. Do you hear me? You had no business messing with her in the first place." She let go of my shoulders and busied her hands with putting the first-aid kit back together. "I knew something was going on between you two, but I never thought—"

"I love Janet, Mom. I would never hurt her."

She shook her head no and pressed her lips together, probably believing I was too young to know anything about love.

I was young, but the idea of me raping Janet was just stupid, and I couldn't understand how anyone, especially my family, would believe it. I needed to see her, for us to talk this out. She had told me she thought she was pregnant the week before, balling her head off so much that I could barely make out what was going on. When it finally came through, I had about five minutes of total and complete freak-out. Then she laid her head on my shoulder and asked me what we were going to do. I hugged her and told her I didn't know, but that we would figure it out. It was the we part that got to me the most. Love had brought us together, and I believed that this little accident would keep us together. Either in marriage, or as dual parents of the same child. Either way was all right with me.

After I asked Mom about Janet again, she told me to forget about it.

"Her parents will take care of her now. You just need to be grateful they're not getting the police involved."

I may have been too young to know what real love was, but I did know blackmail when I saw it, which was exactly what Janet's parents had come over to do. Seeing as I was gone within the week, it worked.

I finished my beer in one big swallow, let out a burp and sat back down. Mom busied herself with the pots on the stove and even though my compassionate sense told me not to, I asked her one more question.

"Did you believe him, Mom?"

She didn't answer me right away. She kept stirring the beans, took a taste and then sprinkled in a little salt. After she replaced the lid and adjusted the flame, she turned to face me.

"Of course I didn't believe him. A mother could never believe her own son would be capable of such a thing."

It was a shallow answer, but probably the best I'd get from her anytime soon. I allowed the cold comfort I got from it to push aside the bitterness and brought myself back to my real purpose in being there in the first place. I apologized and said I didn't mean to cause any problems or upset her. She gave me a half smile, looked like she wanted to say something else, but just folded her lips together instead. A minute later, she excused herself to go check on Dad.

I had a mental argument about going with her, but my bad angel won. I stayed put and told myself I'd go if she called me needing help or anything else. She didn't, and came back about ten minutes later, told me he was doing well, then set the table for our dinner.

The rest of the evening was pretty quiet; both of us did our best to avoid slipping back into our previous discussion. After we ate, I helped her clean up the kitchen and then we watched some TV. We ended up watching reruns and right after *Touched by an Angel*, Bobby came back to help set Dad up for the night. He made me watch, telling me I needed to know what to do. I stood in the doorway and watched as he rolled Dad onto his side while Mom worked on the bed, removing a thick white pad they had under him and replacing it with a clean one. Dad seemed to be drooling and dripping and oozing out of every orifice in his body. They had a pajama top on him but below he was as naked as a baby. I know I made a face when I saw it, but I couldn't stop myself. I could've gone the rest of my life without seeing that, but there it was: my dad's big, black lifeless cock exposed for the entire world to see. It kept flopping around every time they moved him like a lifeless, limp limb he had absolutely no use for anymore. Mom didn't seem too bothered by her husband's exposure, but I noticed Bobby paying a lot of attention to the ceiling. The worst part about it was that they had some little tube going up inside it; a catheter to catch all his urine. It looked pretty painful and I could feel my own dick wince in commiseration. I made a mental promise to Little John-John that I would never, ever, subject him to the same treatment.

The process of changing the pad and settling Dad back in bed probably lasted only about a minute or two, but it seemed like thirty. Mom had on gloves, and she was moving around him like she really knew what she was doing. After he was lying on his back again, she glanced over her shoulder and told me to get a wash cloth from the bathroom. I did as I was told, more because of my need to get out of the room rather than a desire to be helpful. After I handed the cloth to her, she told Bobby and me we could go.

"You get used to it," Bobby said when he saw the look on my face.

"Oh, yeah? I don't think that's something I want to get used to."

After Bobby left, Mom and I spent about another hour watching TV. At ten I told her I was going to bed. I asked her where she had been spending the nights since the hospital bed replaced their old bed.

"I've got a bed set up in the craft room," she said. "I keep the doors open so I can hear if anything goes wrong during the night."

"Why didn't you guys put Dad in Bobby's old room? That way you could of at least had your same bed."

"Oh, that old bedroom suite? I've wanted to get rid of that for years. That mattress wasn't worth keeping anyway, and after." Her voice trailed off and I could only guess at which after she was thinking about—after he went into the home, or the other after. She was staring off into space, so I just kissed her good night and headed to my room.

I hadn't called Pamela, but it was too late by then. Tomorrow, her relatives started coming for the family dinner that evening. Sunday was the memorial service at the church, followed by another graveside memorial. Pamela's dad is the head of the family, and it wasn't one of those unspoken rules that relatives follow. His place of authority was understood, accepted and talked about by anyone who mattered. So when BJ Sprey says they are going to have a memorial service for his momma, they have a memorial service for his momma. Not that he bestowed any special privileges on those that did participate, but everyone seemed afraid of being the one who didn't. After knowing him for almost ten years, I still couldn't figure out where his power came from. He has money, but I only know that because Pamela told me about some stock and land investments he made. Anyone looking at the Sprey's lifestyle wouldn't think they were more than a middle-class Black family making it in Los Angeles. Maybe his people think of him as a big piggy bank and going along with him was just one way to help break him open.

Aunt Idell holds the same place of respect in our family tree. She and her husband built a mini-empire with their appliance stores, and she is known to share the wealth with family members that are in dire need. She was also the one who took care of Dad after his own mother ran off. With whom she ran off with has always been a big mystery. That and my dad's real father. We don't know much about my grandmother, since the only thing Dad would say about her was that mothering wasn't something high on her list of priorities. The last time he saw her he was five only years old. Same age as Jackson.

After I got into bed, I told myself I'd call Pamela first thing in the morning. I also spent a few minutes remembering the stories Idell used to tell me about Dad. They weren't pleasant ones. At least up until she got to keep him for good. She told me more than I'm sure he would have wanted me to know, but it hurt her to see me that angry at him. But I was a resentful, angry, hard ass teenage boy. Even if she had told me my father had been raised by wolves, I wouldn't have budged in my resentment.

•       •       •

That night I dreamed I was driving in an old, long station wagon. I was driving over some hills looking for an exit I needed to take to get to a resort town in the mountains, but I couldn't remember the number of the highway I used to take. I had taken it before, but I couldn't remember the exit number. I thought it was seventy-four or one-seventy-four, but I couldn't remember it or see any freeway markers that would help me. I took an exit and thought about getting a map or asking someone for directions. There was a white couple there with a young daughter who didn't say much. She just moved around a lot and would pop in and out of the scene. The woman showed me a map, and I found the highway I wanted. But when I saw it on the map, I realized that I had been taking the long way. There was another highway, a larger one that went straight through to the town. The one I had taken before was just a thin red, curvy line on the map. The other highway, the one I didn't know about, was straight and wide. The woman told me that I should take that one, but I thought about all the fun places I had passed on the other road. I told her I would think about it; then that little girl was back giving me a bag of apples, a small brown bag with a paper handle across the top. The woman laughed and said that the town was famous for its apples and then she asked me to help advertise them. She wanted to put a bumper sticker on my car, but I told the husband to just stick it on with tape—I wanted to remove it without damaging the paint on my car. Then we were all in their living room and the little girl was sitting next to me handing me apples. She kept putting them in my lap, and I tried to hold them with my arms, but they kept spilling off onto the floor. The couple was sitting in another chair; the wife on the husband's lap. They were making out. This didn't seem to bother the girl. She just kept giving me apples, and then she started showing me all these other things made from apples like apple sauce, apple butter, and cakes and pies, even apple bubble bath. The dream ended when a wooden chair in the room burst into flames. The woman jumped off the man's lap and said, "Oh shit!" She was mad because the chair was made out of wood from an ancient apple tree and she was really upset to lose it. The man picked it up, threw it into the fireplace, and huge, blue flames shot up thru the chimney. I remember thinking that apple tree wood makes a superb fire. Then I woke up.

# Chapter 8

Saturday morning came fast and dawned bright. The house was quiet, but I knew Mom was up by now. She always woke early as if she had a job to go to or something. But her *work* was taking care of the family. Her words, not mine.

The clock on the dresser let me know I had slept almost seven hours, but I was still tired. I shut my eyes and blamed the drive down and the four arguments for my fatigue. That first one with Jamal, then Kim, followed by Bobby, and finally the small one with my mother. I felt the worst about giving my mom a hard time. So much for having a different experience this time. The only difference was that I picked on her instead of Dad. Causing trouble is never my intention. It always seemed to be waiting for me, lurking around the corner like some thug waiting to knock me in the head, grab my wallet and take off.

Before I did anything else, I called my wife. I thought that was a good way to start the day off right, doing my husbandly duty. No answer, so I called the Sprey's house. Her dad answered.

"Hello, Mr. Sprey. This is John. Is Pamela around?"

"Hello, son. How's it going down there? How's Walter?"

"I haven't talked to the doctor yet, but I'll know more later on today."

"Really? Emily sounded pretty upset yesterday. She said the doctors weren't too encouraging."

Yesterday?

Mr. Sprey continued, "Pam said your mom and you and your brother were going to put him in a home this weekend."

"Well … I think that was an option my mom was considering … ."

"Oh … I thought you knew. Pam told me that's what you were going down there for." He felt bad.

"Don't worry about it, Mr. Sprey. Everything is so up in the air right now; none of us really know what's going to happen. Ahh … when did you guys call?" I closed my eyes and prayed it had been while I was out looking at sites, and Mom had forgotten to tell me. At the same time I knew that was impossible. Mom was the best and most efficient message taker I had ever known. Not only would she relay the message, but hours later she would ask if you called back or took care of whatever the call was about. If she didn't tell me, it could only be because ...

"Pamela called right after you got there. Your mother said you were on your phone outside, and that she'd tell you to call us later."

Mr. Sprey was speaking, but my mind was too busy cursing at myself and that stupid lie I told to understand anything he was saying. When something came through that sounded like, "I'll get Pamela," I pulled it together and told him not to bother.

"My mom's calling me; probably to help with my dad. Tell her I'll call in about an hour."

He told me that they were leaving in a bit to go to the church and check on the arrangements for tomorrow.

"Tell her to call me when you're done. Please."

"Of course. And we'll be sure to offer a prayer for your father and the family."

I thanked him and ended the call. All I could do was stare at the cell phone in my hand. My first instinct was to hurl it across the room and smash it into a million pieces. Next, I got mad at Mom for making a fool out of me in front of Bobby. I'm sure I was mad at him, too.

I tried to move into damage control mode, but every option seemed stupid. There wasn't one person I could say I was talking to that would make any sense. So that was that. Caught. In the movies it's always the phone-call-lie that triggers the downfall, so I knew I had to be extra careful from then on. I deleted Kim's phone number, found that note, and tore it into even smaller bits until it looked like confetti. I put half of it into the bedroom trashcan, then slipped across the hallway into the bathroom and dropped the other half into that trash.

The bathroom mirror reflected my face back to me. I didn't like what I saw—a grown man sneaking around like a kid hiding a bad note from his teacher. That morning was definitely a low point of my visit, but not the lowest, and I realized that trouble wasn't really waiting for me. It didn't have to since I had brought it down myself.

While drying off, I decided to store the incident away as more proof as to why I needed to cut the bullshit and get on with the serious business of my life—a seriousness that did not include messing around. My dad lived that way, and as far as I could tell, Bobby was doing it, too. I was supposed to be smarter than them, wasn't I?

I forgot my shaving kit, so I rummaged through the cabinet for Dad's stuff. He's used the same brand since we were kids and the smell of it brought back a thousand memories, mostly from when I was still little and Dad would carry me around on his shoulders. I'd press my baby-smooth cheek against his and squeal over the roughness of it.

I sniffed the mound of shaving cream before smoothing it over my face. When I kissed Dad yesterday, he smelled sour. Like a carton of milk weeks past its expiration date.

Mom put a cup of coffee in front of me as I sat down at the kitchen table.

"Good morning, honey. How did you sleep?" She pushed the sugar and cream towards me before adding, "I guess you slept pretty good seeing how late it is."

I tried to apologize, but she brushed it off.

"Don't worry about it. I'm glad you got a good rest in. You're going to need it these next few days."

I took a gulp of coffee and wondered: Doing what? It seemed like she and Bobby had taken care of most of the grunt work. All I was there to do was offer moral support.

"I'll do whatever you need me to do, Mom. That's why I'm here." I looked up, smiled at her, and she smiled back. In her hands was a bowl of hot, steaming oatmeal. She had arranged the raisins in a smiley face, exactly the way she did when I was a kid.

"I couldn't help myself," she laughed.

We spent the next half hour making small talk and gearing the conversation away from my own family. I didn't mention my phone call to Mr. Sprey, and she didn't ask, but it was hard for me to sit there. I felt guilty. I was guilty, but having it stare me in the face and present me with a bowl of happy face oatmeal was too much. I concentrated on my food and let Mom chit-chat about the day ahead, hoping she wouldn't bring up anything that happened yesterday.

I was just finishing up when we both heard the doorbell.

"That'll be Gretel," Mom said getting up. "She's the nurse that comes around most mornings to check on Dad."

The door opened, and I could hear mom and the nurse talking in the living room. Their voices got louder as they moved towards the kitchen. Glancing at the backdoor, I thought about, but just as quick dropped the idea of making a getaway, and then smiled and congratulated myself on sticking to my new bull-shit free life. It was a premature gesture.

"Johnny, this is Gretel, your father's nurse."

I stood up with a generic and no-frills image of a nurse on my mind—white dress, orthopedic shoes, thick ankles, and an unremarkable face. I was wrong.

"You're the nurse?" I tried not to stare, and to hide my surprise, but damn.

"That's what I told you, Johnny." Mom could see I was drooling.

Gretel extended her hand and said good morning.

"Nice to finally meet you. I've heard a lot about you."

"Nice to meet you, too." My voice purred out like a pick up line, and under any other circumstances I would have slipped into the mood. But since this wasn't a bar, I was at a loss and completely speechless. Mom was staring at me staring at Gretel, and poor Gretel was casting those gorgeous dark brown eyes around the kitchen like she was looking for an escape.

Finally, Mom cleared her throat, "He had a pretty quiet night. I only had to get up once to check on him."

"Check on who?" I asked, my eyes still on this nurse who looked like she had walked off the cover of Ebony Magazine.

"Your father, John." Mom shook her head. "Who else?"

Gretel laughed. My face burned, and I mumbled an apology, and then that silence came back.

Mom broke the spell again and motioned Gretel to the back bedrooms. Gretel rushed out a quick goodbye and walked out. She had what looked like the heaviest bag slung over her shoulder and a thick notebook tucked into the crook of her other arm, but she carried it all like it was nothing. Strong and gorgeous. I was checking out Gretel's backside when I glanced up and saw my mother giving me a look.

It felt like someone had slapped me, but the pain wasn't on my face. That oatmeal churned in my stomach like cement, and all I wanted was a hole to appear so I could jump into it and be gone.

My mom glared at me, her chest rising up and down with each deliberate and pissed off breath. She must know everything now, I thought. She knew about the affairs and the lying. She knew about the phone call and now seeing me act like a dick-headed fool over this woman sealed everything. Any other man would have gotten a pass, a boys will be boys pardon. But not me. Not John Roberts. The boy who raped his fourteen-year-old girl friend, and who leers at his dying father's nurse like a sex craved prisoner.

My only way out of this new fuck-up was to excuse myself and walk back to my room. I passed Gretel in Dad's room. She was taking his blood pressure and glanced up as I passed the doorway. I hurried past and into my room, the only hole I could find.

I fiddled around trying to keep busy while Gretel was still there. Under my bed I found my old Battleship and checkerboard games. Bobby and I used to have a pretty good time with them. Playing board games was the one thing we could do together that didn't end in us trying to kill each other. I put the games on the dresser with the idea of taking them home with me so that Jackson and I could play at night after dinner.

Mom knocked on the door and opened it after I said come in. "Gretel's done with Walter and Bobby's on his way. Can you be ready to go in about twenty minutes?"

"Sure, Mom." She looked past me to the games on the dresser.

"I thought I'd take these home with me," I told her, then added, "If you don't mind."

"They're your games, John. Why would I mind?"

"Well, they're Bobby's, too."

"So ask him. But if I was you, I'd just take them. Bobby has a daughter and she's into Barbie's, not war games."

She started to leave. "Mom?"

"Yes."

"Sorry."

"For what?"

"For whatever, Mom. Let's just call it a pre-apology for whatever screw-ups I do today, OK? Because every time I'm down here somebody—"

"Oh stop, John. We had this conversation last night, remember? The past is over and the only thing you keep doing every time you come down here is re-live it. It's embarrassing and the best thing you can do for your wife, your son, and for yourself would be to forget it all and just move on. We all suffered—especially Janet—but you don't see her or any of us hanging on or holding grudges."

"What do you mean Janet suffered? Her parents took care of her."

"They took care of her all right. No woman is ever the same after going through something like that." She crossed her arms like she was protecting herself from a sudden draft. "Her parents didn't even discuss it with us. Your dad was furious."

Mr. and Mrs. Moore claimed that Janet had a miscarriage a few weeks after my exile to Long Beach. Whether it was natural, or something her father had a hand in, no one will know. Except the people directly involved, which should have included me, but of course it didn't.

"More concerned about his reputation than his own daughter's wellbeing," Mom told me this when she had called to let me know. I was holding on to Aunt Idell's phone so tight I thought it would crack in my hand.

The front door opened and closed, followed by the sound of Bobby calling out for us. Mom told me to be ready and then left. They met in the hallway.

"Where's John?"

They talked for a bit about the day's agenda and other stuff that went right over my head. After the house phone rang and I heard Mom answer it, I came out and met my brother in the hallway.

"How's it going? Sleep well?"

"Yeah. Felt kinda weird being in the old bed again. But I was so tired it didn't matter after a while."

He took a conspiring step towards me. "So, what did you think of Nurse Gretel?"

"She was all right." I said, trying to sound as neutral as possible. "I didn't get a good look at her. Very efficient nurse, though. Came right in and went right to work on Dad."

Bobby's mouth twisted into a yeah, right grin, which I ignored and changed the subject to the nursing homes.

"So, which one we going to first?"

Magnolia Homes was their first choice so it would be that one.

"And then that's it, unless you really object to it," he said.

"Why would I do that?"

"You wouldn't, and you aren't. Mom and I ran ourselves into the ground looking at those places, and if I have to look at any more and smell all those gross old-people smells and pull another creepy, lonely old man's hands off me, I'll go nuts." He shook his head. "The first thing I need to do when this is all over is get my papers in order. I'm gonna let everyone know that if I ever get to this point, just pull the plug and let me go in peace."

"What are you talking about Bobby?" Mom materialized from the kitchen.

"Nothing, Mom. Only wondering when we can get started."

"That was Mrs. Anderson on the phone. She's running a bit late."

Bobby groaned after Mom left. "Well, that will be one good thing to come out of this. No more dealing with inept nursing aides."

"I didn't know you were having trouble with them," I said.

"Nothing serious," Bobby said. "Except that they are either always running late, or they have to leave early. Mom is such a softy, and they take advantage."

I knew they couldn't afford a place like the expensive home Grandma Rose was in, but I imagined my dad staying in one of them, surrounded by a level of luxury and opulence he had always rejected. Even in his half comatose state, he would hate it.

Bobby excused himself and went to the kitchen for a cup of coffee. "No telling how long that woman will be," he said.

I joined him, forgetting about calling my wife. He took the last of the coffee, so I poured myself a glass of orange juice. We sat down facing each other. I asked about his wife and daughter—a safe subject.

"Oh, they're all right. Natalyn will be glad when all this is over. She complains that I'm gone too much." He took a sip. "She doesn't understand a son's responsibility."

She wasn't the only one who didn't understand it. "You've been really helpful to Mom," I told him. "Thanks."

I may have not known what a son's responsibility was, but I did know that I had not been living up to it. Mr. Sprey understood and lived it. Both parents gone, but he still plays the good son. And everybody respects him for it.

Even though Bobby was older, I never thought of him as the responsible one. If I was ever in a situation and thought, What would Bobby do? I'd do the opposite. My older brother wasn't the brightest dude I knew. His grades were always in the C-D range, and the only books he read were the comics which aren't really books at all. He tried to write a 6th grade book report on the Spider Man series but got an F. Dad only laughed about it, claiming that his eldest son was being creative.

Bobby finished his coffee and got up to put the cup in the sink. "Well, like I told you yesterday, Mom and I really appreciate you coming down."

I nodded and finished my juice.

The aide finally arrived. Mrs. Anderson was the same nurse I talked with yesterday, and this time the nurse looked exactly the way I had imagined: an older, heavy-set woman, dressed in a typical white nursing uniform and matching shoes. She wore her black and grey hair in a tight bun on top of her head; her face was brown and smooth, not a wrinkle in sight. She carried a huge canvas bag that had everything in it *but* nursing supplies for Dad. Instead, it was stuffed with tabloid magazines, knitting yarn and needles, a fat book of word search puzzles, aspirin, and enough snacks to feed an entire kindergarten class. She chuckled as she unloaded it all on the table, her huge bosom bobbing up and down.

"Well, I finally get to meet the younger son. Heard a lot about you, John."

Gretel had said the same thing.

"Your mom tells me you a whiz at the real estate game up there in Long Beach. My niece lives up that way. I'm gonna tell her about you because she and those children of hers need to move out of that too small apartment."

She rambled on about how the little ones had to share a room with the big ones and about the landlord who didn't do a damn thing except raise the rent. She seemed to be enjoying her little tale of woe so much that I didn't even bother to explain to her that I got out of the house selling business years ago.

Mom came in with her purse and sweater on. "John doesn't sell homes anymore, Mrs. Anderson. He just deals with those buildings for stores and offices."

She looked me over, up and down. "Well, I'll say. You are into the upper-class stuff, aren't you?"

She acted offended, which seemed like an overreaction to me. Maybe she was upset because I let her ramble on about her niece knowing I couldn't help her. Or maybe she just didn't like being corrected period. She went to put her juice in the refrigerator.

"You all can take off now on your little errands. I got it covered. Spoke to Gretel a while ago, and she told me what to watch out for." She glared at me. "And who."

# Chapter 9

Mrs. Anderson excused herself and left to do her obligatory check on Dad. Her heart wasn't in it because she kept on mumbling about her niece's cramped apartment. I looked at Bobby and Mom for a reaction, but both seemed oblivious to her indifference. After about thirty seconds she wobbled back out to the living room, turned on the TV, and plopped down on the sofa.

"Well, I guess we should be going," Mom said. "Are you ready, John?"

I was still staring at Mrs. Anderson. She pulled out a huge bag of pork rinds and was munching away.

"You want some hot sauce with that? Or maybe a soda?" I yelled to the back of her head.

"Huh?" she said in between the crunch-crunch of deep fried pork fat.

"John. I asked if you're ready," Mom's voice was as loud as mine.

I ignored Mrs. Anderson's questioning eyes and turned to Mom. "I still haven't talked to Pamela. Give me ten more minutes."

"Well, hurry up. We don't have all day," she said, not even bothering to give me the same courtesy she just gave Mrs. Anderson.

Mom disappeared into her room. I gave Mrs. Anderson one more piercing look before heading to my room. As I passed Dad, I turned to peek into the room. His eyes were wide open and looking in my direction. When our eyes met, his chin jerked up at me like we had just passed each other on the street, and he was giving me the *what's up?* nod.

I stepped into the room, hesitated, and then took the few steps to his bed. He was turned on his side with pillows stuffed into the small of his back and behind his knees. His good arm was tied to the bed railing with a strap that looked like something you'd find on a straight jacket. Dad's head jerked up again. His lips opened and a phlegm-filled pant rushed out. He coughed. I looked around for some water or that suction thing Mom had used last night but didn't see either which was just as well because I wouldn't know what to do with it anyway. I looked at his face again. He was working his lips, trying to say something but the words couldn't seem to make it out of his throat.

I leaned over him. "What do you need, Dad? Can I get you something?"

His face held an intensity I hadn't seen since that day of our big fight. But this time his eyes were not lit up with anger. I stared down into his face to make sure I wasn't imagining what I was seeing. The corners of his mouth curved up into a small smile, and I couldn't deny the Santa Clause twinkle in those enormous eyes of his.

I leaned over him again, "What is it, Dad? What do you need?"

The smile faded from his lips as he inhaled and forced out one word: "Don't."

I held my breath and waited for more to come, but it never did. That one word took it all out of him and with his next exhale his body deflated like a balloon.

I put my hand on his shoulder and gave him a little nudge. "What is it, Dad?" He didn't respond. At all.

"Mom!"

Five seconds later she flew into the room, demanding to know what was wrong.

"He seemed really out of it," I said. "It worried me."

She stepped to his side and looked him over. "He gets that way some times." She straightened up and patted my arm. "When he first came home, I had a couple of those moments too, John. The doctor says there is nothing they can do about it. Just have to keep a good watch on him, that's all."

"You mean like Mrs. Anderson is doing now?"

"Don't start with her again. She's been in this business a lot longer than you or me, and I'm sure she knows what she's doing."

"Miss Rose had a full-time nurse and I—"

"Is everything all right?" It was Mrs. Anderson. I wanted to ask her where the hell she had been, but Mom spoke up first.

"Everything's fine. Walter faded out for a second and John panicked."

"Well, they do that now and then." She stepped over to Dad's bedside, squeezing me out of the way. "Not much you can do about that 'cept wait, watch, and pray."

I grunted my disapproval, and both women turned to glare at me. Mom with that warning look in her eyes, but Mrs. Anderson's gaze let me know that she didn't give a rat's bee-hind about what I thought. I ignored both of them.

Yesterday, when I learned how sick my dad was, I experienced that devilish sense of, serves you right, and felt zero guilt. But that morning I saw a man suffering a humiliation as no man should. My father was the man who would spend half the day under some house fitting pipe or cleaning out septic tanks, then return home, mow the lawn, change the oil in his wife's car, and still have enough energy to give his sons the third degree while the family ate dinner. My dad had run a successful business and raised a family all on his own, and I couldn't help feeling that he deserved … better.

I still can't put my finger on what happened to me that day. Maybe instinct told me that being a better husband went hand in hand with being a better son. Or maybe revenge morphed into shame. But what I do know is that all of my childhood fantasies of laughing at his suffering and dancing on his grave vanished. I was a husband and a father with a family to raise and care for, and like most kids I promised that I would do a better job—be a better husband, a better father, a better everything. I worked my ass off and could boast a higher standard of living, but that was about it. I had made a mockery of my marriage vows, and the only thing I had going with my son was a stupid coin collecting hobby. And I was even fucking that up.

"John, are you ready to go?" Mom asked me. "The people at Magnolia are expecting us this morning."

I was ready to do something, but it wasn't going with them to check on this Magnolia Gardens nursing home. If they used the same level of judgement in picking that place as they had for picking this aide, I didn't want to know about it. Mrs. Anderson sucked. And as for Gretel? Well, let's just say that a woman that good looking could be doing a million other things than going around town checking up on old folks. Something was not right with her, either.

When I got to my room, I closed the door and called my wife. She picked up after the first ring. I wasn't even thinking about covering up for yesterday. The only thing on my mind that morning was Dad.

"John? How's it going down there?"

"Not so good," I answered.

"Is he that bad?"

"He's not good, and I'm worried about what they want to do to him."

"The doctors?"

"No. Bobby and Mom. They have it all planned out, and I don't think that would be the best thing for him."

"John, just try to be supportive. This isn't easy for any of them, and I'm sure they don't need you telling them they're not doing it right."

As his son, I felt I had exactly that right. "All I'm saying is that I'm not too sure about this nursing home idea."

"Nobody is ever sure about these things, John. My dad went through hell making that decision, remember."

"Yeah."

"And it turned out all right, didn't it," she said.

"Your grandmother died, Pamela. In a strange place surrounded by strangers." That wasn't true, but I was desperate to make a point. The whole clan had gathered around that woman during her last hours. Me included.

"Everybody dies, John. Our job is to provide comfort so that the end comes with peace and as little pain and suffering as possible."

"And that's the problem. They seem more concerned with their own inconvenience than anything else. That's why they're so hot to dump him someplace."

She was quiet for a while, then said, "That's not fair, John. And it's not true. You know that."

The only thing I knew was that something about the situation was not right, and that's what I told Pamela.

"All I want to do is make sure this home is good enough for him, and if it isn't, then think about other options."

She responded that I just needed to get used to the situation. She said that Mom and Bobby had had more time to process everything. "They probably felt exactly the same way two weeks ago and coming to this decision couldn't have been easy."

"He deserves better."

"That's strange, coming from you," she said.

"He's my father."

"Oh, I know that, John."

"So?"

"So this is the first time I've heard you be so concerned about his wellbeing. This is the same man who you won't even buy a Father's Day card for. The same man who you wanted to kill over a piñata. Remember."

I remembered. "That was before," I said.

"Before what?"

"Before whatever. Look, I just want to help. I can do that, you know."

"The best help you can give is to be supportive and understanding."

"That's all I'm good for, huh?"

"That's all they *need* you for John. That's all."

•      •      •

Magnolia Gardens looked exactly how I imagined it would: dirty and cheap. The lobby had four shabby couches and a few end tables scattered around in the sorry attempt to mimic a normal living room. The residents looked like they were either bored to death or doped up to the point of near unconsciousness. It was Saturday and the number of visitors must have been higher than usual. Middle-aged kids leaned in close to their senior citizen parents and tried to make idle conversation. A few noisy grandkids ran around unchecked, ignoring the glares from annoyed guests.

The lobby was a huge half circle, and from where we stood I could see three wide corridors—one on our right, one directly in front of us and one on the left. Each hallway had a mock street sign over it. There was Daisy Lane, Wisteria Drive, and Magnolia Hall. I looked down Daisy Lane on my left and saw about a half dozen Girl Scouts making their way down the hallway. They were singing what was supposed to be a cheery tune, but they were so off key it was hard to tell. They had these huge handmade tissue paper and pipe cleaner flowers. One young girl stepped up to a crotchety looking woman in a wheelchair and tried to put a flower in her hand. The woman raised her arm as if under attack, and screamed at the girl to get away.

"I want my pancakes!" the old woman shouted.

My shoulder blades cringed together as her screechy voice tore down Daisy Lane and into the lobby. Two aides dashed down the hall towards them. The Girl Scout started to cry and her friends huddled around her for support. An even older looking guy on the other side of the hallway lifted his head in what looked like Herculean effort and told the old lady to shut up.

"Quit talking about those damn pancakes!"

By then the aides, who looked like they could all be related to our Mrs. Anderson, had reached the situation and were trying to calm everyone. They wheeled the woman back to her room, her screechy voice still hollering for pancakes. They wheeled the old man in the opposite direction and as he passed us, we overheard the nurse say, "Now Mr. Allistar, is that any way to talk to your wife?" Bobby and Mom laughed. I didn't.

Mom noticed the troubled expression on my face and started to explain how Dad would not be in this area at all. "Your dad is not able to sit up in a wheelchair yet. He'll mostly be in his room."

"At least for the first couple of months," Bobby said. "They have a physical therapist who will work on getting him to sit up and help get that bad arm working again."

Mom's eyebrows arched up in warning to remind me of the conversation we had yesterday, but the last thing on my mind was protecting either of them from whatever fear or horror they imagined was coming. Pamela was right. Everybody dies, and the best the family can do is make sure the end comes as peacefully and painlessly as possible. They may have settled on this place, but I knew it wasn't the only nursing home or option we had. I saw no reason to not open up the discussion again. A discussion that included input from me.

A short, middle-aged man came up to us from the right. He was wearing tan slacks and a white Polo shirt with the Magnolia Gardens emblem. Underneath that was his name badge: Robert McKinley, Director. He wore his collar up in a style that had gone out in the 80s, and he was wearing brown loafers. The guy looked like he should be relaxing on some yacht holding a strawberry daiquiri, and I would have bet twenty bucks that he and George Hamilton used the same tanning salon.

"Good morning, Emily. I was just about to call and see what time we could expect you." He beamed. "Now I don't have to."

"Sorry I didn't call earlier. Things got a little bit out of control with Walter this morning." Mom said.

McKinley morphed into his care and concern look. "Oh, I understand, Emily." He placed his hand on my mother's arm. "That's what we're here for, to make things easier on the family."

I crossed my arms over my chest, glared at him and said, "My mother, Mrs. Roberts, brought me in to see the place before we make any final decisions."

Mom shot me another warning glance, but I continued anyway. "We are still considering other options." Bobby gave me the same look, and I ignored him too. I had been in that dump for ten minutes and could already tell it was a mistake. I couldn't imagine how Mom and Bobby had even considered it.

Mr. McKinley arched up his hairy eyebrows. "Other options?"

"My son John is just getting in on all that's been going on since the stroke. He's still getting use to the idea." Pamela had said the same thing.

McKinley turned on his care and concern look again. "Of course. I understand."

By the way he sized me up, I recognized a true salesman, being one myself. He believed he had the deal all settled, and then I come along and now he's got to work up a whole new game plan.

"What would you like to see, Mr. Roberts?"

I wanted to see his license, records, and reports from the last decade. I wanted to check the Better Business Bureau and whatever other agencies are responsible for overseeing these places. And I wanted to know why that old lady couldn't have her pancakes.

But Mom answered for me. "We just need to show Johnny the room, that's all."

He started to lead us but she told him it wasn't necessary. "We'll come to your office when we're through."

"I thought I was here to check it out, too." I told her as we moved away from Director McKinley.

"You are, John. But I really can't see what your objections could be. No place will be perfect."

"I'm not looking for perfection. But I think a certain level of competence is not too much to ask for." I turned to Bobby, hoping to get him on my side. "It's what we want, right?"

He didn't answer, just kept walking alongside Mom and me, quiet as a pile of dog shit. He always clammed up at times like this. But I wanted him on my side and for us to work together. I figured it would be easy to stall Mom for a day or two and get her to wait on making any firm commitment to this place. Maybe tell her we should consult a lawyer first or something like that.

There were a lot of reasons I wanted to stall them. I was resentful because they had made the decision without me, and I also thought neither was in the right state of mind to make such a big decision. Both of them told me how worried they were—about each other. Dad was an afterthought.

I also had a bit more experience with these end-of-life issues since I was with Pamela when her family had done the same thing. I knew more about looking up records and checking references from other residents. Mr. Sprey even drove out to Pasadena to the family of a man who had lived at Peaceful Horizons for seven years. A phone call satisfied Mrs. Sprey, but her husband didn't trust that. "We could be talking to the owner's nephew," he had told her.

I turned to them and said, "I know nothing will be good enough, as good as home that is, but let's not set our standards so low that we'll jump on the first thing that comes along."

Bobby spoke. "This isn't the 'first thing,' John. We've looked at about half a dozen places."

"What do you mean, 'as good as home?'" Mom asked. As we made our way down Magnolia Hall, it started to look and feel more hospital-like. Red crash carts, nurses dispensing pills, and the beeps and chirps of monitors filled the hallway. We had reached the doorway of the room they intended to keep Dad in. I peeked in over her head.

"It looks like a hospital in there," I answered her.

"It's supposed to. Your father is sick, real sick. He needs a serious place. Not some over-priced, pointless place that's more concerned with its looks than the care."

Bobby joined her. "You can't really think that Dad could go someplace like Pamela's grandmother was in, do you? Where the hell have you been the last 24 hours, John? Did you even notice the shape Dad's in?"

"I noticed. Have you?"

"Or maybe you've been more worried about other people than your own father," he said.

I took a deep breath and chose my words with care. Bobby had inherited Dad's pride, and it looked like a little of it had rubbed off on Mom, too.

"All I'm saying is that we need to take our time making a decision. And if money's an issue, then that's something I can help out with."

"'We'? Now all of a sudden it's 'we?'" Bobby said. He pointed back and forth between himself and Mom. "Well, *we've* been working and worrying our asses off these past two weeks John, and *we* think it's a little late in the show for you to all of a sudden start caring."

"We didn't ask you down here for money, John." Mom said. "We asked you to come because you're family. His son."

"I know that, Mom. I just want what's best. As any son would."

We had been standing in the doorway to that room for a bit too long, so a nurse came over to ask if we needed anything. She wanted to know if we were there to see the man in the first bed.

Mom explained who we were.

"Oh yes," she said. "Mr. McKinley told me you'd be by. Don't worry about disturbing Mr. Polakava; he's pretty out of it. Can't hear a word we say."

"I read somewhere that that was really not true," I said. "That these patients can hear and understand what's going on around them."

She looked me over the same way Director McKinley had.

"Well, in some cases that may be true. But since Mr. Polakava is completely deaf, along with being comatose, I don't believe he falls into that category." She turned to Mom. "My name is Dana, if you need anything, just come to the nurse's station or push the call button."

Mom and Bobby thanked her, and the three of us walked into the room. Mr. Polakava was lying flat on his back, eyes closed, mouth wide open exposing a set of bright pink gums. He was breathing on his own, every breath an exertion. On the little table next to his bed someone had set up a few family pictures and get well cards. I noticed the same card I had almost bought myself, and the coincidence made me feel more than a little bit creepy. Behind the cards was a 9 by 12 black-and-white photo of a couple at their wedding. The man was tall, with a long lean face, and a strong, straight nose. His hair was slicked back like Clark Gable's, and he even had the thin moustache to boot. His bride was a full head shorter than him. Her head rested on his shoulder; face turned to the camera with a bright smile that left no doubt of her happiness. Her teeth were straight and white. I wondered where she was.

I glanced back at Mr. Polakava. The only sign that the barely alive man in that bed was once the young man in that photo was the hair. It was grey, but it was all there and someone had combed it the same way as in the portrait. If he could have picked which part of his self he would like to have kept in his old age, I'm sure he would have picked consciousness over hair. But none of us get to make that decision.

Bobby and Mom had walked over to the window, and now both of them watched me and waited. Bobby with his big arms crossed, looking impatient; Mom looking anxious. The two of them together threw me. It was always Mom and me. Not Bobby. Especially after the San Diego trip that had paired us together. After that weekend, I never went anywhere with Dad. Bobby was always the one to tag along on his plumbing jobs or to a ball game. After they left, Mom would glance down at me and ask, "Where to partner?"

I wanted to say something to her, but her look of anxiousness seemed to double. So I pretended to examine the room. There wasn't much to see. They had stripped the bed down to the plastic covered mattress, and the only other piece of furniture was the nightstand that sat next to the window. A quick glance out the window showed only a cinder block wall and some very tall and very ugly weeds.

My first impression was that the space seemed too small; just room for the bed and maybe a chair or two for visitors. I took a step towards the call button on the wall. "Let's give this a try and time how long it takes Nurse Dana to get in here." I was only half joking.

"Stop screwing around, John." Bobby turned to Mom. "Are you happy now? Your baby son has seen the place. Now let's get this over with." He started to leave.

I blurted out: "I don't like it." That stopped him. He turned back and glared at me.

"What?"

"You asked me for my opinion, and that's it. I think this place is crap, and I don't want my father put here."

"Oh Lord." Mom tilted her head back and closed her eyes.

Bobby took a step towards me. "*Your* father? You don't want *your* father here, John?"

"All I'm saying is that I think we can do better for the old man. That's all."

"Better? You think we can do better?"

Bobby repeated what people said right before he blew up at them.

"Did you hear that, Mom? Your baby son says we can do 'better'."

Since he was all wound up, I didn't back down. "Both of you know that Dad's days are numbered."

"Oh, Lord." She leaned against the windowsill for support.

"So we should do our best to make his last days as peaceful as possible."

"'Peaceful'? Now you're all concerned about the family peace?" Bobby said.

"Cut the bad-ass act, Bobby. You know I'm right. You told me yesterday in the garage." I turned to Mom. "And you told me practically the same thing over dinner."

She straightened up and glared at me. "I told you that in private, and I expected it to stay that way."

"What the hell's the big secret?" I said. "I came down here to see about my dad, not to protect you two grownups from the inevitable. Look, there is no Santa Claus, there is no Easter Bunny, and people die. Even fathers and husbands."

"What the hell do you know, John?" Bobby said. "You only graced us with your presence a day ago, so now all of a sudden you give a damn."

"A blind man can see how bad off he is. Hell, he almost died right in front of me this morning."

"What?"

Mom took a step forward, putting herself between me and Bobby. "I'm the wife and the mother, and I say this is what's best for everyone involved."

I opened my mouth to protest, but her hand in my face stopped me. "I just can't take it anymore. I can't. Your father can't be at home, and this is the place I've chosen for him. I'm sorry if you disagree, but my mind's made up."

"OK. Again I ask: What's the rush?"

"The rush is you were right. He could have died right there this morning. And that's the last thing I want—or need—is for him to pass away in the house and have his soul haunt me for the rest of my life."

"What are you talking about Mom?" Bobby said. His eyes were wide and sad.

"The only people who want to die in their own homes are the ones doing the dying," she said. "Nobody that has to live in it afterwards wants to have that memory hanging over them." She clutched her purse in front of her. "Plus I heard it brings down the value of the house."

"What!?"

The conversation was taking more twists and turns than I could keep track of. First Bobby was on me, then Mom, and now Bobby and I seemed to be together in our astonishment at the words coming out of our mother's mouth. Her husband was on his deathbed, and she was worried about the price of real estate?

Bobby spoke first, which was good because I was still in shock. "What are you saying, Mom?"

"I'm saying we need to get your dad in here quick because I do not want him dying in the house."

So much for the fragile mom theory.

"Is that all you care about?" Bobby's voice trembled. "Dumping Dad somewhere just to get him out of the house?"

Even I thought that was a bit unfair and waited for her to slap him across the face, but she just turned and stared at him for a few seconds before walking around him to the door. When she reached the doorway, she stopped and looked back at us over her shoulder.

"I'm going to see Jack. You two wait in the car. It shouldn't take long."

Bobby moved to make another protest, but I stopped him. "Just let her go."

He got in my face and gave me the, this is all your fault, speech. According to him, things were just fine before I showed up and that Mom should have never called me. "What did she think we needed you for anyway?"

I didn't know what she needed me for either, but that was beside the point. I was there now and knee deep in it like he was. "I thought you wanted Dad here. Why are you so pissed?"

Big tears started to roll down his cheeks. "Didn't you hear her? No one gives a damn about him but me. I wanted him here so they could take care of him. Maybe make him better. Not just so he could die."

"Look, Mom's been doing this all on her own, so I guess she must be really tired."

"She hasn't been on her own. I've been here too."

"At night? Have you been the one waking up two, three times a night to check on him and make sure he hasn't drowned in his own spit? I didn't see you wiping his ass or messing with that bag of piss."

Silence.

"Exactly. Mom needs a break, that's all. They call it respite care or something like that."

"I know what they call it, but she's not talking about taking a break for a few days."

I threw up my hands. "What's wrong with you, man? So what? You were all for this when you thought she was against it. But now you see she's for it and you get all I'm the only one that cares on everyone."

"What about you? A minute ago you were calling this place a dump."

"It is a dump."

"Well?"

"Well… I think I have a better option."

He waited.

"I think he should come stay with me and Pamela."

Bobby started to laugh, but what came out was a sort of half-laugh. "You are truly something, brother. Where in hell did you get an idea like that?"

"From Dad."

# Chapter 10

Bobby stormed out of the room, leaving me alone with Mr. Polakava. I turned back to the window and stared at the cinder-block wall and contemplated what I said, why I said it, and how to either make it happen or back out of it. I told Lisa that a white supremacist had a better chance of getting in my house than my own father, and Pamela was right about all the animosity.

The last time I saw my dad was at Cholé's seventh birthday party. Natalyn was in the middle of a suburban house wives' pissing contest, so they had to outdo all the neighbors with this party. They rented a jumper, had pony rides, a magician and hired a catering company. Cholé wore a mermaid costume. The party's theme was sea life, and Jackson looked cute in his pirate costume. Natalyn called us weeks before to clear dates with us, so skipping it was out of the question. Besides, Jackson enjoyed himself. Up until piñata time.

His grandfather had volunteered to take over that task. Dad slung a rope over the branch of a huge tree in the front yard and hung the piñata there. It dangled, a huge starfish, in the wind.

Piñata time came, and about twenty little kids lined up to take a whack. Dad stood off to the side, holding the other end of the rope, and had a blast pulling that starfish up and down and moving it from side to side. Little kids swung like crazy, and most got at least two or three licks in. Then it was my son's turn.

Jackson was one of the smallest kids present, so I felt my dad should have given him a break. But Jackson swung that stick about twenty times and all he hit was air. My dad was laughing his ass off, shouting things like, "Swing harder!" and "Pretend you're hitting your dad!" After a minute, his turn was up and Jackson took off the blind fold and slinked off to the sidelines with the other kids.

I was cool, though. Just stood by, waiting and watching. No one looking at me could tell that a storm of fury was raging inside. No one except my wife. She had been watching too, and right before the last kid burst the starfish open, she pulled me aside and told me to be cool.

"Did you see that?" I said. "He embarrassed our son. On purpose."

"It's a game, John. Your father was making sure every kid got a chance, that's all. Just let it go, please."

The kids were screaming with laughter as a shit load of candy spilled onto the grass. I saw my son scrambling with the rest, shoving loot into his pockets. My dad was in the fray too, grabbing candy along with the little kiddies.

Jackson ran up to us, his pockets bulging and his hands full. "Look at all this candy, Mommy! I got a lot!"

After cake and ice cream, the adults sought refuge inside the house and away from all the kids amped-up on sugar. Dad started laughing when I came inside. "Your boy swings like a girl, John. Why don't you bring him down on the weekends and let me show him how it's done."

I stepped up to him. "He would have hit it if you hadn't kept it up so high."

"It's a piñata. You're supposed to make it go up and down. I couldn't go easy on him because he's my grandson." He clapped me on the back like we were two buddies having a beer and talking about the Angels. "Bring him down more. I'll teach him how it's done."

Both our wives were observing and probably praying too. I took a step closer to him, bringing us chest to chest, and I was just about to tell him off when Pamela intercepted.

"John, Natalyn needs you to run to the store for ice." She tugged at my arm until I had to go with her. My father was oblivious to my feelings, but before he could say another word Mom distracted him, too. Something about them needing him outside for pictures.

I never found out if Mom and Dad talked any more about it, but it was all *I* talked about on the drive home. As soon as Jackson fell asleep, I started. I accused my father of everything from backstabbing to sexism. Pamela just listened. Finally she asked, "So what, John? Your father is your father and there's not much you can do about it."

"There's a lot I can do about it."

"Like what?" She crossed her arms and waited. Our conversations over my father always ended this way. She asking me what I could do about it, and then I'd respond with a bunch of bullshit answers like say we'll never see him again, or that

I'll confront him—eventually. Neither ever happened, and I'd return to fuming and my building resentment.

Standing alone with Mr. Polakava in what was supposed to be my father's future home, I realized that two things happened while I had been busy fuming and feeling resentful: My son would never get a chance to have his grandfather show him how it's done, and Bobby slipped into my place beside Mom.

Mr. Polakava snorted through his open mouth, and I walked over to his bedside. His face held a peaceful expression, and he smelled fresh, like a load of clean laundry.

I'll never know what my dad had tried to tell me that morning, but it felt important, whatever it was. He said, "Don't," but don't what? Don't let them take me? Don't go away? Don't let me die? Don't ever bet on the Detroit Lions? Who can say? But it wasn't what he said; it was more of how he said it. The yearning was pretty clear, and what else would someone in his position want? Or not want.

Maybe Dad never told me anything, but what bugged me the most was that everyone thought the only thing I was good for was moral support. That John Roberts could actually do something seemed impossible to the people who were supposed to love and care about me the most.

"I wish you had kept your sorry ass up in Long Beach." Bobby said right before he stormed out of the room. "After all this time you still know how to fuck things up with your stupid ideas."

I continued to stare at Mr. Polakava and wondered who, if anyone, ever came to visit him. He startled me when his head jerked to the side, as if an invisible hand had pushed it there. It didn't stay put for long and rolled back to its original position. The raspy in and out of his breath stopped. His chest became flat and still. I looked around for his call button and was about to run out for help when his breathing came back. He inhaled and took a deep sigh, like he just got through pondering the world's most complex issues.

No one came in to check on him, and I didn't bother to inform anyone about what happened. Dana hadn't been too concerned about him. To her he was probably just someone they had to pop in on once or twice a shift. It wasn't like he could go anywhere or roll out of bed like a frisky toddler. I know most nurses are overworked and underpaid, so they tend to take the easy route whenever they can. I didn't want them taking that attitude with my dad, and I was sure they would.

I made my way towards Mr. McKinley's office and arrived just in time to see Mom shaking his hand goodbye. Bobby was nowhere around.

"There you are," she turned to me. Underneath her left arm was a maroon colored folder, bulging with paperwork. "Where's your brother?'

"No idea," I answered her.

Mr. McKinley couldn't hide the smug look on his face.

"Your mother and I were just finishing up." He reached out to pat her back, and it took every ounce of effort on my part not to reach out and rip his arm off. "Your mother has quite the head for these insurance matters and such."

"Oh yeah?" I said. "You been holding out on us, Mother?"

"Well, Rob does such a good job of explaining everything. All I had to do was sign my name." She touched the folder under her arm. "I'll have to look over these more closely at home."

I pressed my lips together and didn't bother mentioning how she was supposed to read the docs before she signed them. I turned towards the lobby.

"Wonder where Bobby went off to?"

Mom looked me over. "What happened?"

"Nothing."

"Nothing?"

"He stormed out right after you did. I guess what you said upset him. A little."

"I didn't say it to upset anybody. It just had to be said, that's all."

McKinley cleared his throat. "If you don't need anything else, Mrs. Roberts, I'll be leaving you two now. I'll make all the arrangements for the transportation. Don't worry about any of that."

"Not until Tuesday like we talked about," Mom told him.

He winked, "Got it."

Jesus Christ. "Why Tuesday?" I asked.

Mom watched him walk away before answering. "Some family wants to come by the house before he leaves."

"Like who?"

"Like family, John. Maybe Idell. Does she know you're here?"

"No, I had to leave—"

She gave me her I-don't-believe-you look.

"What?" I shrugged. "I'm a busy man, Mom. I used to see her all the time, but then with Jackson and work and … you know."

"Well, you'll be seeing her soon. When can Pamela and Jackson get down here?"

"Slow down, Mom. What's your rush?"

She didn't answer, and headed back towards the lobby. "Where in God's name is that brother of yours?"

We spent about two minutes roaming the corridors of Magnolia Gardens but came up empty. "Do you have your phone? We need to get to the bank, not messing around here with you two grown men."

I didn't bother to remind her that Bobby, the reliable one, was the one messing around.

"He's probably out in the car," I said.

She took one more look, her head turning to do a quick survey of the area. "Well, let's go then." We walked out of Magnolia Gardens.

Bobby wasn't waiting in the car, but he wasn't far away. My phone rang.

"You guys done in there?"

"Yeah. Where the hell are you?"

"Across the street at the coffee shop."

I looked over and saw him sitting at a small table with a big dark green umbrella over it. He said, "Tell Mom to come over. We need to talk."

"I'm not telling her nothing. Get over here so we can get going."

"What's he doing over there?" Mom followed my gaze. "Tell him to come on."

"Mom says to come on."

It was almost twelve with the sun high and beating down on us. Its glare off the passing cars only added to the heat of the afternoon. I shielded my eyes with my hand and looked at my brother across the street.

"Look man, it's too hot for this. Just come on back and we can talk in the car." Then I whispered to Mom. "Maybe we should go and see what he wants."

She pressed her lips together tight, which was her way of saying no. No, and I'm so mad I won't open my mouth because I'm afraid of what will come out. It was that kinda no.

"Bobby, Mom wants to go to the bank now. We can talk in the car."

"I'm leaving." Mom said.

I shut my phone and waved my hand for Bobby to come over. I felt like a traffic cop and doubted he would obey my hand signals right after he ignored a direct order from our mother.

"Wait in the car," I told her, not realizing she was nowhere around. "I'll go over and see what's up." I didn't stop for an answer, but started towards the coffee shop. I was about to step off the curb when I heard the car's engine start. I turned around just in time to see my mother pulling out of the parking space. She pulled up beside me and I tried to open the door, but it was locked.

She yelled at me through the car window.

"You and your brother need to work out whatever it is needs working out. I'm too old and too tired for this. Call me when you're ready to be picked up." And then she sped down the street and turned right at the next corner. I jogged the short distance to the corner and watched her drive to the end of the block, stop, signal left and turn. Then she was gone.

"Momma!" I hollered like a kid who just got dropped off on his first day of kindergarten. When it sunk in that she wasn't coming back, I had a mild fit of stomping, kicking and cussing. Bobby had finally pried his big butt from the chair and was staring down the empty street, too. I stormed over to the coffee shop ready to pounce and beat the crap out of him.

"Look what you did," I yelled, pointing an accusing finger down the empty street. "She left us, you dumb-ass."

"What did you say to her?" he asked me.

"I didn't tell her anything. It was you and your, 'let's talk over coffee' bullshit." People were staring at us, but I didn't care. "You need to grow up, man." I pulled out a small metal chair and sat down. He looked at me for a bit then sat down again.

"Did she say when she'd be—"

"She told me we need to work out what needs working on."

"Maybe she's right," he sighed.

"Look brother, I didn't come down here to mess with you. I came to take care of my dad. And that's exactly what I plan to do." I searched up and down the street. "Is there a bus or taxi that comes by here?"

"Why? You got an appointment? Or a date?"

"Shut up. You *do not* want Dad in that place. Well, neither do I, so we need to work together to see that that does not happen."

"It doesn't matter, you know. Mom's right. He's gonna die any day now. He might even be dead right now; we just don't know it because Mrs. Anderson is too busy watching TV and stuffing her face to notice." His voice came out all wobbly and his fists were clenched tight. His bottom lip quivered like a baby's.

"Hey man, calm down, all right. Let's just get out of here and not make Mom any madder than she already is?"

A single tear rolled down his puffy cheek. "My father is dying, John. And I, unlike you, give a damn about that." He grabbed some dirty napkins and started wiping his face.

A woman at the next table handed me some more. "Is he all right?"

I took the napkins. "Yeah, he'll be okay. We just got some bad news about our father."

She tilted her head towards Magnolia. "Is he over there? I worked there for a while. It's not a bad place to be your final days." She sipped her coffee. "I've seen plenty of people leave this earth in much worse situations."

I thanked her and turned back to my brother. He had pulled himself together, but it was a struggle.

"Are you gonna be all right, man? We need to go catch up with Mom and get things settled."

He stared at me, his eyes still teary. "Didn't you hear her back there? Things *are* settled. She's sticking Dad in that place so he can die."

"Well, what did you think? That she was putting him in there to play shuffleboard and learn line dancing."

"Fuck you."

"Look, you were the one who told me that Dad was in worse shape than we thought. Remember?"

"I know what I said, but I didn't think that she... that she." He flung his hand out like he was swinging at a gnat.

"What? That she would know what she wanted to do, then do it? Maybe you've underestimated her all along."

Seconds passed as he eyed me, then said, "When did Dad tell you he wanted to stay with you?"

"He didn't exactly tell me that," I said. "I just got the idea watching him this morning."

"Watching him do what? Did he say something to you?"

"No ... no. Nothing like that. He just had this look in his eyes, you know ... like he was begging me to do something."

"To do something?"

"Yeah."

"But you don't know what, exactly."

"Not exactly, no."

"And you came to the conclusion that this 'something' was to haul him off to Long Beach—away from me and his wife—and take care of him up there."

"I am his son. Not some stranger, you know."

"His son who hasn't said a dozen words together to him since … forever."

"So does that make me incompetent to take care of him?"

"Incompetent, no; delusional, yes."

"So a son who wants to take care of his father is delusional? What does that make you?"

He leaned back in his chair and matched my stare. "Why do you always have to complicate things?" He shook his head. "That was the one thing about you that drove Dad crazy. John and his stupid ideas and questions and shit."

"Since when is curiosity a crime?"

"It's not. You just never knew when to quit; always pushing and pushing until he would explode and go off on you."

"Dad never got on me for asking questions," I said. "But he was on my ass for everything else, that's for sure."

Bobby looked out at the passing cars for a while then said, "Our father ruled with an iron fist, that's for sure." He was smiling.

"That's funny to you, man?"

He stared at me for few seconds then stood up. "It's not funny. It's over." He grabbed the mess of napkins and his paper cup and threw it in the trash. "Let's go," he called over his shoulder. He weaved his way through the tables and headed down the sidewalk. I got up to follow him, mostly because I didn't know what else to do.

I was silent, not knowing where he was going or what he had in mind. I just followed, like an obedient younger brother. Not so much out of a desire to be obedient, but more because I had no other choice. The neighborhood was unfamiliar and, more importantly, I needed time to think things through.

We walked along, side by side, both of us quiet with only the occasional car whizzing by, and a few noisy birds that flew from tree to tree like they were following us, waiting for the next big scene to unfold.

After we reached the corner, he stopped and looked around.

"She turned that way," I said. "Where do you think she was going?"

Bobby shrugged, "Probably to the bank out on Olive and Main."

"Far?"

"Far enough. I'm not walking there. Shit." He looked at me. "What did she say?"

"Mom? She said to call her when we were ready."

"Ready for what?"

"Hell, I don't know. Ready to get along, I guess."

A dog barked, sending our bird audience flapping off into the sky.

"Look, man," Bobby said, "the only thing I asked you to do was be cool. Remember?"

"I was cool. I don't know what made her snap like that."

"Did you get another phone call? From Pamela."

His fingers did the quotation marks thing around her name. I knew immediately where he was going with that and decided to diffuse it right then and there. "All right, so everybody knows I wasn't talking to my wife. Big deal. It's nobody's business who I was talking to. I didn't come down here to get the third degree over my personal life, so just drop it, all right."

"If you want people to believe you've changed, you have to actually change, you know."

OK, I thought. I tried. I had enough of trying to get along with him, so I looked up and read the street sign on the corner. We were at Lincoln and Ontario. I took out my cell and dialed 411.

"Who ya calling? Her?"

I was going to get a taxi, go back to the house and start making phone calls. I thought Aunt Idell would be a good person to start with. She had connections all over the place and would be the one to know where and who to start with getting my dad up there. She would love it too, having her Walter close again.

"I need a taxi company," I told the operator. "Anyone in Crown City. Try Yellow Cab," Every city has at least that. Bobby chuckled.

"She knows, you know," he said.

The operator connected me to the cab company. I gave them my location, groaned when they said it would be about 30 minutes, and then hung up.

"Mom doesn't know. I haven't told her yet," I said.

"Not Mom. Your wife."

"How could Pamela know? I just told you."

"Not about Dad and your crazy idea. Your wife knows you're stepping out on her." He folded his fat arms across his chest and stared down at me. "And with that stupid phone call and your freak-out when Janet came by, you confirmed Mom's suspicions too."

"What the fuck are you talking about?"

"Pamela started dropping little remarks last summer about you and all your mysterious business meetings. I guess she thought since I had gone through that with Moondera, I could relate."

"What did you tell her?"

"Not what I wanted to tell her, that's for sure. Especially now that I know you're back with her. So how long you been sneaking out?"

"None of your damn business," I answered.

The smug look on his face increased. "Well, since you want to take my father up there, I guess it is my business now. How will you find time to look after Dad with all your other ... ah-hum ... activities going on?"

Bobby and I stared at each other for what seemed like an hour. But it wasn't like before, with Tyrone. Bobby would never understand me.

"Just because I want to help our father does not give you the right to poke your big ass into my personal business. My activities, as you call them, are none of your damn business."

"It'll be all my business if you get Dad up there and then your wife finally comes to her senses and leaves you. Who's gonna take care of Dad then?"

"Don't worry about my marriage. And Dad will have a nurse, just like he does down here, except she'll be a competent one. Where did you guys find that Mrs. Anderson anyway? From an ad hanging up in the grocery store or somewhere?"

"I'd let a hundred Mrs. Andersons take care of Dad before I'd let you do it."

"You don't know anything," I whispered to him, then walked away. He didn't follow me. I rounded the corner and kept on. The area was a lot quieter than the street Magnolia Gardens was on. In fact, it possessed that creepy kinda quiet we used to call earthquake weather, when the air and the time seemed to stand still. I kept walking and felt like I was the only thing alive on that street with its cookie-cutter houses, dark green lawns and meticulous flower beds. Stopping would have been a smart thing to do, since I had no idea where I was going, and getting lost would have made me look really stupid. Or stupider. But I could handle that. What I did not want to do was stop and contemplate what my brother had just told me.

•      •      •

I first stepped-out on Pamela when Jackson was about four months old. It took a year longer than we had planned for her to get pregnant. At first, the baby-making sex was great. But when the months tick by without results, she started to panic. We never sat down to talk about it together—as a couple—and Pamela refused to see a doctor. She just read every book and article on the subject, and then relay to me how we were doing it wrong, or not at the right time, or my briefs were too tight, or how my diet was off, or anything else meant to place the blame on my baby making abilities, which didn't make sense. She knew all about Janet.

She became so anxious and tense that making love to her was like screwing a mannequin. But that wasn't the worst part of it all. The thing that hurt the most was that she refused to discuss it with me. Every time I brought it up, or made a suggestion, she would shut me out and say she had it under control.

If she had just given me the chance, I would have told her that it didn't matter. I would always love her. We could forget about it. We could adopt, be foster parents. Anything she wanted. But silly me, I had assumed disappointing her husband was what was bothering her most.

My first dalliance happened at a three-day conference in Sacramento. It was our last night, so a couple of us were whooping it up in the hotel bar. A pair of females walked in, gave us all *that* look, and then twenty minutes later I'm racking up my bar tab buying strawberry daiquiris, tequila shots and spicy buffalo wings, and laughing at Ted's stupid jokes.

An hour later I excused myself to take a piss, and Ted followed me. He said, "Look John, I know this is your first time, so let me tell you how it works."

I thought he was going to show me how to pee.

"What happens on these business trips is strictly confidential, all right? If the wives happen to ask—which they never do—we hung out at the bar, talked shit, then went to bed. Got it?"

I was at the sink by then, washing up. "What are you talking about, Ted?"

That was funny to him. "Look, those ladies are hot. And just drunk enough to know what they're doing. If we wait too long, they'll pass out as soon as we get them up to the room."

I caught on and wasted no time climbing on my moral high horse and telling him exactly what I thought. "Ted, you can't be serious? We're married. I love my wife. Don't you?"

"Yes, I love my wife. But that's beside the point. Look, if you're not into the moment then fine. Just remember what I told you."

I had only met Ted's wife once, and she didn't look like the kind of woman who would put up with a cheating husband. Pamela wasn't that kind of woman either. Did that woman even exist?

"Ted, you just do what you want to do, okay, and leave me out of it."

He looked at me like I had just folded with a Royal Flush. "Have it your way, buddy." He reached in his jacket pocket and pulled out a travel size toothbrush set. After he finished, he grinned at himself in the mirror, breathed into his hand, and smelled his breath. He turned to me. "How do I look?"

I didn't go back to the table, just passed by, told them all goodnight and went up to my room. I wanted to call Pamela, but she was staying with her folks because her dad insisted she not be alone with Jackson so soon after he was born. I thought it was a bit of an overreaction, but said nothing. Why bother? When she finally did get pregnant, and announced it at the family Thanksgiving dinner, she was looking at her dad, not me.

I was checking out the mini-bar when she knocked. It was the brunette. She told me she had to come up to thank me for the drinks. She was tipsy and leaned against the door jamb for support. Her dark brown hair sprouted out of the top of her head like a fountain and cascaded down to her shoulders. A wig from the Tina Turner collection, I later found out. My eyes traveled down her body. She was wearing a tight black dress that was cut deep in the front. Her breasts bulged out of an even tighter lacy red bra like a pair of cantaloupes aching to be plucked off the vine. She had a small waist and a big ass, and would have looked perfect hanging off the arm of any rap artist. On her feet she wore a pair of shiny red pumps. Three-inch heels.

"Who told you my room number?"

She straightened up and tugged at her dress. "Your friend. He left with Sharon and then there I was, all alone." She pouted and frowned. "Aren't you gonna invite me in?"

The next morning I was in the gift shop when Ted found me. The sales clerk was showing me a silver chain with a heart pendant. I was looking it over when he stopped me. "Why don't you just tattoo I cheated on your forehead?" he said.

When I got home, I was a nervous wreck—jumping at every question and holding my breath each time the phone rang thinking that woman had tracked me down. Every time my eyes met Pamela's, I'd swallow hard and look away. Not only was I a cheating husband, I was a wimp, too.

The weeks turned into months and Pamela never acted like she knew or even suspected. At first I was shocked thinking how dense she must be to not even be suspicious. Or maybe I was that good?

• • •

I kept walking and was turning corners and going down streets without a clue as to where I was headed. I was hoping to come upon something familiar, but when I moved away this area was covered with sorry looking orange trees, and plenty of tall weeds. My phone rang. It was Bobby, and I surprised myself by answering.

"What?"

"Your taxi's here. You coming back?"

I read the street number of the house in front of me and told him to tell the cab to come pick me up. Minutes later it pulled up with him in the back seat. I got in.

"We're splitting the fee," I told him.

Bobby just grunted and gave the cabbie our home address. "The bank's closed by now," he said before I could ask. "Hopefully, Mom's back at home waiting for us."

I settled back in the seat, gazed out the window and hoped she wouldn't be too upset. The last thing I needed right then was to get in another argument with her. Pamela and my mother were the two most important women in my life. I didn't want to lose either of them. Yes, I knew that cheating on my wife was the one sure way to lose her, but that was always one of those thoughts I could easily push to the back of my mind. Way back. My mom would always be my mom, I knew that, but the idea of her hating me, being ashamed of me … it was too much to think about.

The cabbie kept glancing at us in his rearview mirror, probably nervous as hell over the obvious tension radiating between two black men. I was nervous, too. My great secret was never any secret after all. Bobby knew, my mom knew, and now he tells me that Pamela's known all along. Jackson might even be a little suspicious after my great Minnesota quarter fuck-up.

I turned to him, "Look, what you said back there was true, all right? But that's all over now. I decided a while ago to cut it out." I wanted it all cleared up between us before we faced Mom again. I hoped he would be on my side.

"So what was all that with the mysterious phone call?" he asked.

"That was one of the reasons why I'm through creeping around. These women just get too intense sometimes."

He laughed. "Thanks for that little brother. For a moment there I thought you actually grew a conscience or something. You're not supposed to quit fooling around because it's become inconvenient. You're supposed to quit—well not even start in the first place—because it's wrong."

"Don't preach to me. Okay? As far as I'm concerned it's old news. Like I said, I'm done, and no one needs to know anything else about anything. All I want to do now is focus on taking care of my dad."

"You should tell her," he said.

"What? Are you fucking crazy? Why would I do that?"

"You're the one claims you're turning over a new leaf. A flat out confession would be just the thing to get you started out on the right foot."

"It would be just the thing to get some hot grits thrown on me. What the fuck's wrong with you man? If you're so sure, and Pamela does know, why hasn't she said anything, huh?"

I answered my own question. "I'll tell you why. Because she doesn't want to know, that's why."

He shook his head. "You're one crazy messed-up brother, and you better watch it. Your luck may be just about ready to run out."

The cab driver laughed, startling us both. He had pulled up to our house. Mom's car was in the driveway and there was a black Saturn parked on the street. "That'll be $16.75, gentlemen."

Bobby reached for his wallet and gave the man a twenty. "Keep the change."

The driver laughed again. "Thanks. You know, if you don't mind my saying, your brother is right. I had a cousin who decided to fess-up to his wife, and she cut him up so bad he needed twenty stitches and two pints of blood." He folded the money and put it in his front pocket. "They're still together though. Go figure."

Bobby opened the door. "Thanks man, but we can handle it from here."

He wasn't done. "You know why they say let sleeping dogs lie? Because if you wake 'em up, they'll tear your balls off!"

# Chapter 11

As soon as we walked in the house, we knew something was wrong. We didn't see anybody, but heard voices from Dad's room and the kitchen. Mrs. Anderson was in the bedroom with Dad, and Gretel had returned. She was on the phone in the kitchen. They didn't hear us come in.

"Yes, doctor," Gretel said into the receiver. "I'll let them know. Thank you."

Bobby and I stood there, not knowing where to go first; both of us frozen, afraid of what was coming.

Before we could move or say anything, Mom came into the living room. I tried to read her face for a clue as to what was going on, but all I could make out was calm. "Oh, there you are," she said.

"What's going on?" Bobby asked.

She took a deep breath. I held mine. "It's nothing serious, honey. He's running a fever, that's all. Mrs. Anderson called Gretel, and she came over to double check."

"What's the doctor say?" I asked.

"To watch him through the night and call him back if it gets too high."

"What's too high?"

"One hundred two degrees," Gretel answered. She had slipped up behind Mom. This time I couldn't help but notice her confidence and professionalism over her good looks. Just her presence seemed to calm us all down. She put a reassuring hand on Mom's shoulder. "Don't worry, Mrs. Roberts. This is pretty typical stuff for patients like your husband."

I felt bad about doubting her earlier.

Mom wrapped her arms around herself and nodded quietly. "How did you two get home?" she asked us.

Bobby and I exchanged looks, both of us waiting for the other to speak first, like we used to do when we were kids gearing up to talk our way out of a broken window or vase or some other childhood infraction.

"Well," she said, her voice full of impatience. Gretel mumbled something and excused herself.

Bobby opened his mouth, but I interrupted, "We took a taxi. After we talked things out. Everything's cool now, Mom. Promise."

She eyed me, then looked to Bobby, and I could feel a bunch of unspoken words pass between them, like telepathy or something. She was giving him a chance to add his take on the situation. What I had said wasn't a lie, but I was selective with the details, and I know she could tell there was more. After about half a minute, I braced myself, thinking he was about to crack under her gaze, but he just sighed and nodded.

"Yeah, Mom. Don't worry about us. How's Dad?"

Gretel and Mrs. Anderson talked in the kitchen while the three of us made our way to Dad's room. He looked the same, maybe a bit more tired, if that was possible. Bobby sat down in the chair next to his bed and held his hand.

"He feels warm," he said.

Mom put her arm around his shoulders and reminded him what Gretel said. Then she told him he should go to his own home.

"Natalyn and Cholé will be missing you about now. It's Saturday; you should be with your family."

He mumbled some excuses as to why he should stay, but Mom wasn't buying it. After five more minutes of Mom telling him to go, he finally stood up to leave. Keeping his eyes on Dad, he said, "I guess I could go and check on the Chaffee's kitchen remodel. And Natalyn wanted to take Cholé to the park to practice her soccer."

Mom nodded her approval. "That's what he would want you to do, Bobby. Don't worry about us. John knows how to take a temperature, and a nurse is on call the rest of the night."

He left right after the nurses, but made me walk out to his truck with him. I was glad we were alone, I wanted to thank him for not telling Mom everything, but he stopped me before I could get it all out. "Just stop messing around, John. Mom needs you now, and so does Dad."

"I know what to do, Bobby," I said. "You're not the only one who cares, you know."

He gave me a yeah-right grunt, got into his truck and left.

After he drove away, I hung outside for a while and gazed up and down the street of the old neighborhood. It was a weather perfect Saturday afternoon, but it hardly resembled my childhood Saturdays. Back then the streets and sidewalks were filled with bicycles, skateboards, roller skates, and Hula-Hoops. In the summer, we could usually get a pretty good street ball game going, and we played outside all day long, coming inside only to eat or pee. The street lamps were our timekeeper. But with all the kids grown and gone, the street was static and serene, like a pod mall with way too many vacancies. With the parents holding onto their houses, no young families with children had a chance to move in. It would probably stay this way for a while.

I leaned on the trunk of Mom's car and wondered what Pamela and Jackson might be doing. She was my go-to person. Not Kim, not Terry or whatever that other one's name was. But the idea of talking to her scared me. *She knows, you know.* That super-secret life I thought I had built was turning out to be not so secret after all. Tyrone had figured it out, and he's not what anybody would call bright, so I had a hard time dismissing what my brother told me about my wife knowing. And then there was Mom.

My mind rambled on until a list formed of all the people who may, or may not, know. The Definitely Knows list was too long for comfort. It had the women, a few odd motel clerks, Bobby, Ted, and that cab driver. Tyrone was on the Maybe Knows list since his evidence was all circumstantial, nothing that couldn't be refuted. Pamela, and Mom, and everybody else were on the Maybe Knows list, too. The only loose cannon I could think of was my brother and he, out of everyone else, would be the one to get all righteous and screw things up. I could beat him to it and confess to Pamela like he wanted me to do. Or, I could take my chances and pray he'd keep his big mouth shut. Neither option appealed to me.

So this was my situation: My wife may have discovered my indiscretions, my dad was in danger of taking a turn for the worst, my mom was pissed, and Janet was still out there and within reach for the first time in almost two decades. I just wanted to talk to her, but with everything else going wrong, I wasn't in a position to do something like have an innocent reunion with my first true love, even though Pamela knew the whole history. After I had told her, I asked her if it would ruin things between us. She hugged me and told me it wouldn't. She thought it was very honorable how I had wanted to stand by Janet.

"Most boys your age would have run," she had told me.

The only other time Janet Moore had come up in our marriage had been right here in Crown City, and in my bedroom. We were here for my brother's wedding, in which I was supposed to be his best man. This was actually his second marriage. The first wedding had been a Justice-of-the-Peace affair that I missed. He had married his high school girl friend, Moondera Wilson. They got married within a year out of high school, and then she left him six months after that. She was pregnant, but not by my brother. When the divorce papers came, he signed them, got on with his life, and a year or so later, started seeing Natalyn, a girl three years younger and in her final year in high school. But he didn't marry her right away. Just got her pregnant, shacked up with her for two years, and was finally doing the right thing as my mother liked to call it.

The first thing that happened when we arrived home was Pamela and I walking in on an argument. An argument about me. Mom wanted me to be Bobby's best man, but Bobby had already asked his best friend, Tyrone Williams. When Pamela and I arrived, Mom had to do some fancy talking to smooth things over. She told me she hadn't known about Tyrone and had just assumed that the brother would be the best man. Bobby started to mumble his apologies too, but I cut him off and said it didn't matter.

I told him, "Your best man is supposed to be your best friend, right?" That quieted them both up.

So that was event number one. Event number two happened the same night. Pamela had spent the day with Mom, shopping and taking care of some last minute wedding stuff. As we changed for bed, I asked her how it went with Mom.

"It was nice to get to know her some more. We've only talked on the phone, you know." Then she asked, "What did you and Bobby end up doing?"

"Not much. We talked a bit. Then he had to go catch up with Dad at a job they needed to finish before the weekend."

"Did you guys talk about the wedding anymore?" Pamela asked.

"What's to talk about?" I answered. "It looks like Natalyn and her family have everything set to go. The only thing left is to say 'I do' and then you and I can say 'goodbye' and head back to Long Beach."

"How long are you going to carry that grudge around, John?" she asked. Dad and I had barely said ten words to each other over dinner. She sat down on the edge of my old bed.

"You sound like Mom," I told her. "She's always telling me to move on, to 'Forgive and forget' she says."

When I sat down next to her, she put her hand on my knee. She had her nails done that afternoon with Mom, and the dark red polish stood out against the dark brown skin on my leg. She smoothed her hand up and down my thigh and said, "She's right, you know."

I was getting turned on, so I moved away from her and stood by the dresser. She was wearing a flannel nightgown that I'm sure she got from her grandmother. It came up to her chin, and down to her knees. Very respectable, but it still turned me on.

I took a deep breath and answered her. "Look, it's not me, it's him. It's this place."

"John, this is your home."

"It's not that I don't love them. I'm their son. I have to love them. It's just that I don't—"

"Like them," she finished for me. "You've told me this before, John." She got up and paced the floor. "But now that I've actually met them ... I don't know."

"Don't know what? If I was telling the truth or not?"

"No, not that. Don't get mad, honey. I'm just trying to understand, that's all."

"Understand what? I told you everything."

She looked at me and waited, and all of a sudden I felt like a little kid being interrogated by his mother. I half expected her to say I couldn't have any dessert until I fessed-up.

"What did my mom tell you today?" I asked, wondering how much Mom may have contradicted my own version of the story.

"She didn't tell me anything, John. I expect your mother has more sense than to tell me her family's business."

"So what is it then?" I sensed there was more. And I was right.

"You've been acting so different since we got here. I can't help but think that there's more to it than just this." She took a deep sigh, and she looked like she was ready to cry. I took a step towards her, but the next sentence out of her mouth stopped me cold. "Are you still in love with that girl, John?"

It's at times like these when a man needs to choose his words carefully. The right answer, of course, was no. But I knew if I blurted it out too fast she would think I was lying. If I waited too long, she would think I was unsure. So I waited a few seconds, walked over to her, took her hand in mine, and looked down into her face. I wiped away the tears from the corner of her eyes. She closed them, and I gently kissed each lid. I told her that the only woman in my life was her. I told her how I felt like a man reborn since she came into my life. I explained how since I'd met her, all my decisions were designed to make myself a better man and, hopefully, a great husband and father.

She tried to pull away from me but I held her close. Then she asked, "What about Janet? I'm worried."

"I'm not going to stand here and lie to you. I'm not going to tell you that what happened between Janet and me is completely forgotten, because it's not. But what I can tell you, what you have to believe, is that I care only about you, Pamela. Right here, and right now. You are the only woman that matters to me."

She began to cry, and I knew I had her. I wasn't trying to get over, or play her along or anything like that. I was genuinely trying to save my relationship. Losing her would have killed me, so I did a little damage control and convinced myself there was no real harm in that. I did care about her a lot, and I knew the loving her part would come soon enough. Just not right then because the last time I'd declared my love to a girl in this house all hell broke loose. Maybe I was trying to protect myself from that again.

We talked a bit more and then went to bed. If we hadn't been in my parents' house, I would have made love to her until she screamed out Jesus' name, and then kept on until she screamed out His mamma and daddy's names too. As it was, we ended up cuddling, which is just as good for most women anyway.

Pamela fell asleep before I did, and as she laid in my arms my mind wandered back to Janet. I had driven by the Moore's house after she left with Mom, and I felt guilty as shit for doing that. Was I still in love with her? Hell, I didn't know, but I knew I didn't want to be. That was the last thing I wanted.

•       •       •

Mom was still with Dad when I went back inside. She was sitting by his bed in the same chair Bobby had occupied. A reassuring smile greeted me, and I decided to apologize for what happened at the nursing home.

"I know you're sorry, and I know you don't mean half the things you say. But sometimes you just go too far."

Too far? If they could hear everything I didn't say, everything I keep inside, then that criticism would be an accurate one.

But I was tired of defending myself, so I forced my thoughts to something else. Like leaving. Getting in my car and going back to Long Beach. Now that would have been going too far, and a week ago it's what I would have done—fled and used the free time to hook up with Kim or someone else. But just thinking about that brought back that nauseous and creepy feeling of despair and insecurity.

It's true what they say about how we only want what we can't have, because right then I wanted—needed—to have my wife with me. Now that made me feel good. I imagined her long and slender arms wrapped around me. I would bury my face inside the nape of her neck and breathe in her scent until it invaded every cell of my body. She would cling to me like she used to, and whisper she loved me over and over again. I would lift her soft, full breasts to my lips and—.

"John!"

I snapped back to see my mom watching me.

"What's wrong with you?"

Mom didn't wait for an explanation. She got up and told me she was going to lie down. "You need to stay here and look after your father," she said. "If you get hungry, there's plenty of food in the refrigerator."

"Yes, ma'am." I took the seat she vacated. Dad's breath had calmed a bit, and he looked pretty at ease, like he was taking an afternoon nap. He was breathing through his open mouth, his lips were dry, and his tongue looked twice its normal size.

They had him on his back, covered in only a thin, white sheet. The last thing I wanted to think about was my dad's penis, but that's exactly the image that came to my mind. Maybe because my own was just beginning to calm down. The chances of my father ever having sex again were pretty much next to nothing. Would he miss it? Would Mom? Pretty soon the yuck-factor took over, and I turned my thoughts to other things. Like lunch.

I put together a ham sandwich, grabbed some chips, and ate in front of the TV. Dad always refused to pay for cable, so the choices were pretty limited. I had nothing to read, no one to call, and was soon bored out of my skull. Thirty minutes passed like three hours.

Relief came after another half-hour passed because it meant checking his temperature again, which was at least something to do.

Mom left the thermometer on the night stand. It was an electric one that gave the results in less than a minute. I laid it on top of his tongue and waited. After a few loud and rapid beeps, I took it out and looked at the reading. ERR blinked like a cheap motel sign.

I pressed the reset button. My error was leaving his mouth open, I knew that much, but telling him to close his mouth wouldn't work, so I laid the thermometer under his tongue again and pushed his jaw shut with the tips of my fingers. His short whiskers were thick, brittle, and stung the tips of my fingers.

I held his mouth shut around the thermometer and waited. It eventually gave one long beep. 99.7°. The last reading was 100°. I wrote it down on the chart, cleaned the thermometer with an alcohol wipe and put it back in its case.

His mouth popped opened again. He looked like a wino, the kind people walked past quickly, head down or eyes averted to avoid eye contact. And my fingers still stung from the hair stubble.

I pushed the button on the remote to lift his head to the upright position and laid a towel over his chest. In the kitchen I found a medium-sized bowl and filled it with warm water. I put that on his night stand then went to the bathroom to get his shaving supplies.

The flesh on his face was flabby and loose. I pulled each section as taut as I could and ran the blade down, slow and easy. I did his left cheek first, then the right. I pushed his nose up with one finger to get at his upper lip. After each stroke, I straightened up to looked at my handiwork, and rinsed the blade before doing another one. The bowl of water filled with the tiny specks of cut whiskers, and my father's familiar face began to emerge. His facial hair used to grow like a werewolf's, and he would sometimes shave twice a day. I never understood why he hadn't grown a beard and be done with it.

After the last stroke across his chin, I used a warm, damp towel to wipe away the leftover cream and inspected him for any nicks or scrapes. None. I smiled at my achievement and then felt his cheek—soft as a baby's ass.

After cleaning everything up, I went back to his room and sat by his side again. I never spent much time in here when I was a kid because it was strictly off limits. With their king size bed gone, the room felt empty. The only other furniture Mom had kept was their long dresser and the other nightstand which was covered with medical papers and supplies. But the dresser looked the same. Mom's jewelry boxes and perfumes were still in place. Dad's side had a few old bottles of after shave and a couple of ties hanging from the mirror's edge. Pushed up against the mirror on Dad's side was a cigar box covered in Popsicle sticks; a gift from me. Mrs. Bryant, my third grade teacher, had us paint the sticks brown before we glued them on. They were supposed to resemble little logs of wood. Some of my classmates went all out and added glitter or rhinestones to their projects. I kept mine simple knowing Dad was not the flashy type.

"It's a valet," I told him on Father's Day morning. I rhymed valet with mallet. "You're supposed to use it to put your wallet and stuff in at night."

"A valet for my wallet," he smiled, turning the box over in his hands. "Thanks, son."

I walked over to the dresser and lifted the valet's lid. His keys, wallet, and some change were inside. Dad's stroke happened as he and Mom were finishing dinner. He always showered and changed before they ate in the evenings, so he must have put his things in less than an hour before the stroke. It was most likely one of the last things he did.

I wasn't surprised he had kept my childhood gift; it was the idea that using it had been one of his last physical acts that unsettled me. I sat there and hoped he would remember the shave as my last contact with him, and not my telling him to go to hell at Cholé's birthday party.

I lowered the lid, looked up, and for the second time that day, caught a reflection of myself I did not like. John Roberts. Son of Walter Roberts. Husband to Pamela Sprey. Father to Jackson B. Roberts. And a complete and selfish asshole.

# Chapter 12

After Mom woke from her nap, I stuck around the house playing it cool and being the dutiful son. She needed boxes put up in the attic, a few door knobs tightened, a sprinkler head changed in the front yard, and something was wrong with the washing machine. The spin cycle wasn't spinning right. I took care of everything except that. Bobby would have to handle that one.

Dinner time was pretty quiet until she brought up the bank. I was doing my best to avoid it, but that elephant was not going to be ignored. She let out a heavy sigh. "Everyone at the bank was so nice. Your father and I have been there since before you were born, you know."

I knew. Crown City National held both their accounts—the family account and the business one. Idell and her husband Jimmy banked there, too. She had told me Crown City was the only bank willing to give them a loan to start the business. She's been loyal ever since. I had been inside that bank at least a hundred times. A little boy clinging to his mother's hand as she waited in line. Bobby would hold on to her other hand and both of us would be as quiet as altar boys because we knew there was a reward waiting for us at the teller counter—a Safe-T lollipop. Two if we were especially good.

"Did you get done what you needed to get done?" I said.

She shook her head. "No. And you'll have to stick around until at least Monday so you can go down there and sign the signature cards. Just ask for Mr. Allen. He'll be expecting you."

"I wasn't—"

She cut me off. "I don't want to hear any excuses."

I set my glass of water down with more force than was necessary. "I was going to say I wasn't planning on leaving Monday. Or Tuesday for that matter."

That settled her a bit. She relaxed her shoulders. "Good."

When she got up to clear the table, I got up too and helped her.

It felt good being useful. I also kept checking in on Dad. Old wisdom says, once a man, twice a child. Walter Roberts the man had been a difficult person for me to connect with, but that Saturday I began to imagine how I could build a connection with this Walter Roberts. He wanted to say something to me that morning, and with therapy I believed he would regain some of his speech. And then we would talk, have real conversations about important things. We never did that before. Our interactions before were always him talking and me listening.

Sunday morning brought a layer of low clouds and the haziness matched my mood. I still hadn't abandoned the idea of bringing Dad to Long Beach, but a plan needed to be worked out before I broached the subject again with my mom and Bobby.

I made my bed then fortified myself for the phone call I couldn't put off anymore. She was waiting, and I didn't want to disappoint her. But all I wanted to talk about was Dad and getting him up to Long Beach. The two of us working together could bring us closer. Plus, she would view me as a loving and supportive son, not unlike her own father.

I sat down on the only chair in my room and called the Spreys.

"John," Pamela sighed after I told her what I wanted to do. "When I said supportive, I didn't mean for you to take over. What did your mom say?"

"I haven't told her yet. And I'm not taking over; I'm trying to help, that's all."

I could imagine her face. She had just let out a long breath through puckered lips, and her eyes softened around the edges as she tried to figure out the best way to let me down, like she was telling our son how chocolate milk did not come from brown cows.

"Let me think about it," she finally offered. "We can talk more when I get there."

I wasn't encouraged. "Pamela, I know you don't think I'm right about this, but I am. You have to … ."

"I have to what?" she wanted to know.

Trust me. "Nothing," I told her instead. "You're right. I won't say anything until you get here."

Her face probably changed to a look of puzzlement. Why the quick switch? She was wondering. "Thank you," she said after a pause.

"You're welcome." The silence that followed reminded me of our first date; both of us all formal, shy and awkward.

"So … how's everything up there?" I said. Always a good conversation starter: her family.

"Oh, good. Everybody is here, starting to get a little sad. Daddy bought Jackson a new pair of shoes to go with his suit and now he wants a red tie, just like Uncle Travis. Mark and Paula's baby girl is a cutie. She has Grandma Rose's eyes." She continued on in the same vein with me only half-listening, which was better than cutting her off with a, I have to go lie. "So, I'll leave right after the memorial," She said. "We should get there around four."

"Great," I told her. "I miss you." I closed my eyes and waited for her to return the sentiment. Nothing. Just a mumbled goodbye followed by, "I'll see you when I get there," then silence as the phone was disconnected.

Just like Saturday morning, Mom was up before me and in the kitchen. She handed me a cup of coffee as I sat down, then set a plate of bacon and eggs in front of me. I waited for her to join me, but she kept on fidgeting around the sink.

"Dad looked pretty good, didn't he?"

"Yes, he did, thank God." She turned around and took off her apron. She was wearing a light blue dress with stockings and short heels.

"Did you bring a tie and dress shirt?"

"No, but I always keep one in the trunk of the car. Why?" I asked, hoping she would say we were going to the theater or something.

"Church."

"Do I have—?"

"Yes, you have to. Hurry up. Bobby and them will be here soon. We'll leave as soon as the Sunday nurse comes."

Fifteen minutes later, my brother and his family arrived. I was fixing my tie when I heard the front door open. I grabbed my jacket and joined them in the living room.

I hadn't seen Natalyn in a while. She was a short woman who had the curse of carrying every extra pound in all the wrong places. She possessed small breasts, a big middle, and huge calves. She liked to wear high heels, low-cut blouses and short skirts. I guessed mom liked her well enough, but I could tell some things bugged her. Like the way she dressed.

I turned to Cholé. She looked like an African-American Oompa-Loompa. Short, round and dressed in a red and white jumper dress.

"Say hi to your Uncle John."

She didn't, and clutched her mother's hand like she was drowning. She was eight; almost three years older than Jackson.

"That's all right," I laughed. "It's been a while." I bent down to be eye-level with her. Her dark brown eyes with long curly lashes reminded me of my son. "My boy Jackson will be here later on," I told her. "The two of you can play, OK?"

She stuck her thumb in her mouth and mumbled an OK. I stood up. "She's cute," I told my brother.

"Yeah," he said.

I looked him over. His suit was well made, and it fit him perfectly. He looked good, so I told him so.

"Thanks," he said. "I had two suits made last year, we being a church going family and all."

"I told him he needed to treat himself," Natalyn said. "Bobby is an important member of the community, you know. Business owner, on the church board … ."

I nodded. Natalyn certainly seemed to be the right woman for him, which was good after his first marriage imploded before the ink had time to dry on the license. Seeing his small family all together, I couldn't help but admit that they looked good, like they belonged together.

Mrs. Anderson had Sundays off, and the nurse who walked through the door was much younger. She wore a white dress, thick white socks, and white Nike's. Her eyes were bloodshot like she had either been up all night or had a hangover. It was the former.

"I just got off my shift," she told Mom. "Three aides called in last night so they made me stay over." She held up a liter of Coke. "But don't worry, this'll keep me going." She took a swig, followed by a huge burped.

Mom hustled us all out the front door and towards Bobby's minivan before I could say anything. I would have much rather stayed with Dad and let that one go home.

"She knows what she's doing," Mom said over my protest. "Besides, we won't be that long."

When Bobby and I were kids, Mom would take us to a small non-denominational church on 4th Street. She always wore white gloves and small round hats. Dad came with us maybe once a month. The pews were hard and in the summer we sweated like pigs in our wool suits.

That small wooden building was gone, and in its place stood a humongous stone and glass structure. The worship hall was a separate building and feeding off of it were three other structures. Bright, white steps led up to the church entrance.

"This place sure has changed. Where'd they get the money for all this?" I said.

"It's not always about the money, John," Mom said.

"All I'm saying is that this church was just a shack last time I saw it. I'm surprised that's all."

"A new deacon came in a few years ago and charmed donations out of every black business owner in the neighborhood," Bobby said. "Including our father."

"No shit."

"Surprised the hell out of me, too. There's a brick over there somewhere with his name on it."

"Damn."

"Will you two watch it? Don't forget where we are," Mom stopped right in front of us. Natalyn had headed off in the direction of one of the side buildings. She had Cholé with her. Mom looked at Bobby, "You're not ushering today are you?"

"I traded with someone."

"Usher? You? Really?" I said.

"Yes. Me. Really," he answered. "I'm a family man now, John. Helping out at church is all part of the game."

"Isn't a game," Mom told us. "Bobby and Natalyn are serious about bringing Cholé up in the church."

She didn't say anything about how Pamela and I had stopped our weekly church-going, but she didn't have to. The look she gave me said it all. This was one area she and my father-in-law agreed upon. And also one area where Pamela had not tried to please her father. She never seemed too anxious to go back to church either, and I never pushed it. About every five weeks, we drive up to attend church with the Spreys. I always believed that was enough church-going for one family.

"Cholé is older than Jackson. We're waiting until he's a bit more mature," I said.

She didn't respond to my weak excuse and proceeded up the church steps. Bobby and I followed her, and the childhood memories came flooding back.

"Hello, Emily. How's Walter?" The usher at the front door handed each of us an Order of Service.

"He's doing pretty well, considering," Mom answered her. "Will you and Steve be able to come by later? He'd love to see you."

She avoided my mother's eyes. "We'll try," she said. "Sometimes getting out after church is kind of difficult."

Mom nodded and thanked her.

As we made our way down the aisle and into an empty pew, I scratched Mrs. Usher-lady and Steve off the guest list. Every salesman knows that we'll try is pretty much the same thing as no.

I leafed through the Order of Service. The topic of the sermon, along with the hymns to be sung, were listed on the inside pages. On the back page was a spattering of ads for local businesses. Roberts and Son Plumbing was listed, and so was Moore Drugs… and More. Their ad was the biggest, taking up almost half the page. I wondered how much that set them back.

When the organist started up, the congregation stood and began singing. The church choir entered the sanctuary through the back door and came down the aisle. There were a whole bunch of them, and it was quite a show watching a sea of maroon colored robes march down the aisle. Their voices rang out strong and full of reverence. I didn't know the song, so I checked out the choir members, hoping to catch a familiar face. I recognized a couple of girls from high school, and then at the very end I saw Mr. Jeff Moore, marching and singing along with the rest of them. He was just as tall and skinny as I remembered, and his face still had that high forehead and short afro. He was looking around checking everyone out, exactly like always, and when his eyes landed on me, he smiled big and waved without missing a beat.

As the choir reached the altar, one line walked to the left, the other to the right. Each thread went to the far side of the stage and made their way up to the choir seats. They met in the middle. It was well choreographed and looked like something you would see on Broadway. Or Vegas.

When the music ended, everyone sat down and waited for the main event. The pastor was a young guy who had a booming voice and shook his fist for effect. Every amen and Praise God was echoed by the congregants. Bobby was pretty stoic through it all, but I heard Mom echoing an amen or two.

Church usually drags like the devil for me, but that Sunday service came to a close pretty quick. People began filing out the front door, and I looked around to see which way the choir went.

"Who you looking for, John?"

"I want to catch up with Jeff."

Mom exchanged a look with Bobby, then told him to go with me. We both protested.

"Just go with him. He might get lost," Mom said.

I would have argued some more, but I did not want to miss Jeff.

We walked to the back of the church and left through the same side door the choir members had. The door opened to another, smaller parking lot and I turned just in time to see a few maroon robes walking around the corner back towards the church courtyard. I followed them with Bobby right behind me.

"You know what she means by 'lost' don't you?" He said. "She's worried you'll get around those two and start to feel all nostalgic and stuff. Forget why you came here."

"Jeff and I were pretty tight," I said. "All I want to do is say hi and see what he's been up to."

"You don't need to see him to do that. The Moore's life is an open book down here. Ask anybody. His father ran off with his dying wife's nurse, the stores are making more money than ever, and the three of them still fight like cats and dogs."

I kept walking. Bobby wasn't telling me anything I didn't already know, but I wasn't interested in town gossip.

We turned the corner and found ourselves in the back courtyard. He saw me first.

"Well look who has finally come back to town." Jeff walked up and wrapped his long, skinny arms around me. He was laughing. "Man, aren't you a sight for sore eyes. Jamal told me he saw you at the store yesterday. You should have come back to the pharmacy and said hi."

"Sorry, man, but I had to get home, you know," I told him.

"Hey, I know, man. Real bad times. Real bad."

It had been almost twenty years since I'd seen Jeff, but it only took half a minute for us to morph back into our familiarity. He asked about my wife, my son, my job, and smiled real big after every response.

"John Roberts: the family man with a house, a career, and a son. Man, you've come a long way, huh?"

"I've done all right."

There was a hell of a lot more I wanted to say, to ask him, but with my big brother standing right there, I couldn't, so we continued with the small talk. I talked the most; he listened, nodded his head and laughed a few times. Not laughing *at* me, but more like an, I'm so happy for you type of laugh. Then Bobby tapped me on the shoulder. He pointed to the other side of the courtyard. Jamal and Janet were walking towards us.

Jamal strode towards me like a freight train, and I found myself backing up into Bobby when he got close. He shoved his hand at me and said, "Sorry about what happened, man. I was surprised to see you, that's all."

I shook his hand. "That's all right. I guess I overreacted, too."

Bobby was looking at both of us with raised eyebrows until Janet filled him in. "John stopped by the store Friday, looking for a card." She smiled up at me, her eyes sparkling behind her glasses.

"A card?" Bobby said.

"Forget about it," I said. The last thing I wanted to do was re-live any part of the last two days. "It doesn't matter anymore."

Jeff clapped me on the shoulder. "That's right, brother. The past is over and as the Good Lord says, Blessed is the man who perseveres under trial, because when he has stood the test, he will receive the crown of life that God has promised. And you, my brother, have surely stood the test." He hugged me again. "God Bless you."

Jamal stepped in between us. "Church is over, Jeff." he said. Then to me. "Look, we were wondering if you would like to join us for lunch. At our house."

Bobby answered for me, "Thanks, but we have to get home. Our Dad is in pretty bad shape."

Janet stepped forward. She was wearing a pale pink dress that showed off her slim waist and full hips. "Oh, we know that, Bobby. How is Mr. Roberts doing?"

"You saw him yesterday, remember?" Bobby told her. It sounded like he was telling on her, and it turned out he was. Jamal turned to glare at her, reminding me too much of Mr. Moore and those looks which always meant trouble was coming. I felt like a teenager again. Janet, though, did not back down.

"I wanted to see him and Mrs. Roberts," she said before he could ask. She squared her shoulders and looked him right in the eye.

Jamal stared back and drew himself up to full height. They faced each other like two bulls, one waiting for the other to charge first. Jamal blinked first, right after his brother stepped forward. "Thank you, sister for going by and giving Mrs. Roberts our blessings. Mom would have liked that."

At the mention of his departed mother, Jamal relaxed his stance, gave his sister one more look, then turned his attention back to me. "Look, we just want to get reconnected, that's all. I know now may not be the best time, but think about it, all right."

Janet was still glaring at him. Her face was twisted into a snarl of defiance, and she looked like she wanted to tear his head off. It wasn't a look that flattered her, and like my last night with Kim, I felt like I was seeing all her unattractive parts for the first time. Janet and Jamal never got along as kids, and almost two decades seemed to have made both of them even more stubborn, with Jeff still taking on the role of peace negotiator.

The courtyard was beginning to thin out. People passed us with a quick glance, probably wondering about this infamous group from the past reassembled again. Most had a white Styrofoam coffee cup in one hand, and a few clutched a sugar doughnut in the other. I recognized the older faces of some childhood acquaintances. Our eyes would meet, then widen when the recognition came through, but then they'd take in the twins and Janet and move on without saying a word. I couldn't tell if they were too scared, or too polite to interrupt.

Jamal had said reconnect, and I allowed myself to imagine what that could look like. Would it be just an occasional phone call to catch-up and shoot the shit, or would it go deeper? Family barbeques at the park; adding them on the people-we-must-see list at Christmas and Thanksgiving; Jackson calling them Uncle Jeff and Uncle Jamal? But where would she fit in? Aunt Janet?

That last thought shined a light on my present reality, which was supposed to be taking care of my dad and acting like the married man I was. Do that, I reasoned, and everything else will fall into place. But them approaching me was a distraction. I had already decided reconnecting would have to wait, but I hadn't expected them to extend the olive branch first. The idea was tempting, and to tell the truth, I was glad my brother had been there to keep me honest. But then he opened his mouth.

"Not anytime soon," He told Jamal. "John's wife and son are coming and other family will be coming round too. Our dad is not doing too well you know." Bobby put his arm on my shoulder and squeezed. "We need John with us right now."

He didn't need to overdo the show of brotherly love. I shrugged out of his grip, not bothering to remind him how he had hurled the opposite sentiment at me yesterday.

"Let me see what I can work out," I told Jeff and Jamal. Janet was standing right by them, but I kept my eyes off of her.

Jeff answered. "Your brother is right John, and if you can't come by our place, then I'm sure your mother will not mind us coming over to offer a prayer for your dear father." He raised his long arms to the heavens and shouted, "Worship the Lord your God, and his blessing will be on your food and water. He will take away sickness from among you."

The surrounding people smiled and cheered him on. "Amen, brother! Tell it!"

Jamal stepped forward and nudged him out of the way. "Church is over, Jeff."

He took my arm and guided me away from Jeff and Janet. Bobby followed us. "Look John, we know you're up to your ass in all this sickness and nursing home shit. Hell, we just went through the same thing." He shook his head. "All I'm saying is if you happen to have a spare hour or two, give us a call. OK?"

All I could bring myself to do was take his offered hand and nod in agreement. He nodded back and returned to his brother and sister.

"What was that all about?" Bobby asked me before we reached the parking lot. "Why are they so eager to get you alone?"

"No one said anything about getting me alone, Bobby. They just want to talk, that's all."

"Talk about what, John? You knocked up his little sister and were sent away. What's there to talk about?"

I grabbed his arm and stopped him. "I know that's all you thought it was about, but you don't know anything. Never did." I pointed back to the courtyard. "Those guys were more like brothers to me than you ever were."

To my surprise, he didn't get upset by what I said. "Oh, I knew that," he said. "The Three J's, right? But let me ask you this: As their *brother*, shouldn't you have known better than to mess around with the *sister*?" After my too long silence, he said. "Exactly." I let him walk ahead of me to the parking lot.

•          •          •

Bobby slapped a sick and disgusting slant on what I meant. He never understood when we were kids and getting older had made him even more closed-minded. I only hoped he would be more understanding when Cholé came to him with her first love. Nothing hurts more than having your parents tell you that you don't know your own feelings.

Janet Moore was the first love of my life, and not the teen-aged, trivial crush everyone tried to reduce it to. I loved her, and she loved me. The first time I told her, the words rushed out of me so fast that I was sure she hadn't understood. Especially because she didn't say I love you back. She made me wait almost a whole day before she returned the sentiment.

We were walking home from school, taking the path we had mapped out that would give us the longest time together and the most privacy. She told me just in time because I was beginning to worry, thinking I had made a fool of myself. She was quiet for most of our walk, answering my questions with as little detail as possible. That really freaked me out because our conversations were what I loved the best about us. We talked about everything—how my dad and brother ignored me, how she was tired of her brothers treating her like a baby, how she didn't want to go into the drugstore business, how I'd rather eat worms than be a plumber, and how hard it would be for both of us to break away from our families' expectations. But her silent treatment that day made me feel like my love declaration ruined everything.

We were almost at the place where we had to go our separate ways, and I was ready to get away from her so I could run away somewhere and kick myself in the ass, but then she leaned into me and whispered, "I love you too, John."

I felt like flying as a wave of relief washed over me. I kissed her right there, not caring who might see us. After that, telling Janet Moore I loved her rolled off my tongue like I was born to say those words to that girl.

About a month after we started seeing each other as secret boyfriend and girlfriend, Janet began to drop some serious hints about how she wanted us to go all the way. I wanted it too and told her how I fantasized almost every night about us doing it in some romantic locale with satin sheets and soft music. She told me she dreamed the same fantasies but didn't want to wait.

"I can't believe I'm the one trying to do the convincing, John." She laughed at me, but I didn't get mad. It only made me love her more knowing she wanted me as much as I wanted her. "My dad will never find out," she continued. "My friend Cara has this secret place she does it with her boyfriend, and she said we could use it anytime."

Cara Powell was the neighborhood slut. Everybody knew that and the last thing I wanted to do was take love making tips from her. "Janet, everyone knows about Cara's 'secret place'. It's the ball shed at the park. Her brother works there and leaves the door unlocked for her at night." I shook my head. "They say that her parents know, but don't care."

"I wish my parents were like that," she said.

I knew Janet clashed with her dad but wishing for the Powell's as parents was a bit much. "I love you, Janet, and I don't want to do anything to ruin things between us. If your father found out, he'd kill me."

She couldn't say anything because she knew I was right. When I would ask her why he didn't like me so much, she never had an answer. "It's not you. It's any boy. Dad doesn't want me to date or have any fun. He says all I need to worry about is school and that's it."

"He doesn't know how smart you are," I said, putting my arm around her. We were in a back alley, inside an unlocked car. Janet started complaining again about how her dad wanted her to volunteer as a Candy-striper at Crown City Memorial. When she first mentioned it a few weeks ago, I loved the idea because I could sign up too, giving us the perfect opportunity to see each other more. "Who cares if it's at the hospital," I said.

"Ohhhh, that would make him sooooo happy," she said.

"What's wrong with that?" I wanted to know. Keeping Mr. Moore happy was what I was going for, but she seemed intent on just the opposite. "Besides," I continued, "this isn't about him. It's about you and me being able to see each other more." Then I held my breath and asked, "You want that, don't you."

Janet didn't answer me with words. She cuddled up to me, put her arms around my neck and kissed me. A soft kiss, but the desire behind it was unmistakable . She pulled away a bit, moved her lips to my ear and whispered, "You know what I want, John."

•          •          •

We were driving home in silence until Mom asked about what happened with Jeff. I tried to tell her nothing happened, but Bobby felt inclined to paint a complete picture for her.

He told her the twins bickered, and that Janet had to set Jamal straight. His words oozed with sarcasm, and he couldn't keep from smirking.

"Jamal kept asking John to drop everything and come over to their house, just like before." He continued. "They still think they run things around here, even after everything that's happened."

"They've been through a lot," Mom said. "You can't blame them for wanting to get things back to normal."

"They want to talk, that's all," I said.

"You know, I never understood why they always thought they were so much better than everybody else," Natalyn offered, even though no one asked her opinion. "They just own a drug store. Big deal. And Janet? Whew! My sister and I used to see her running the streets all night long."

Mom shot Natalyn a warning glance to hush her up, but she hadn't been the first one to talk about Janet and her so-called wild days. Bobby used to call me at Idell's teasing me about who his girlfriend had seen Janet with, or what Janet had been caught doing—his way of rubbing in the fact that I was no longer in town. I would have to explain to him how the only way his girlfriend could have known about Janet's running the streets would be if she had been out there running the streets too.

"The Moores never thought they were better than anybody," I said. "And I should know."

Bobby's hollow laugh rang through the minivan. "Yeah, you of all people ought to know at least that much."

Mom intervened before I could tell him to go to hell. "That's enough, Bobby," she said. "The last thing we need to do is get into it over that family."

We avoided talking about the Moores again while Natalyn and Mom listed all the family and friends that promised to stop by the house. The two women talked about whether they had enough food and drink and ended with Natalyn volunteering to make a grocery store run.

"Just make a list Mother Roberts. I'll take care of it."

The aide surprised me by still being awake. We walked in to find her taking an armload of dirty sheets to the washing machine.

"You back already?" she said.

I guess time flies when you're juiced-up on soda pop.

# Chapter 13

After three hours of shaking hands, hugging, and answering the same damn questions, I was done; 2 o'clock, and time to call it quits. My brain hurt from trying not to think about my wife, Janet, or what I wanted to do for Dad. Plus, Mom was still giving me the cold shoulder every time I tried to bring up Magnolia or other options.

"I said all I'm going to say about the subject," was the only response I could get out of her.

She and Natalyn had whipped the house in shape and laid out enough finger food to feed every relative and acquaintance within a fifty-mile radius.

I recognized most of the people who came by, the family members and neighbors. A few of Dad's business associates dropped by, too. He would have hated for them to see him like that. They all stood over his bed with fake smiles and said,

"You look good, Walter." Or,

"The old guy's still putting up a fight."

It was like a wake for a live person.

Everyone asked when Idell was coming and acted surprised when I told them I didn't know. It wasn't as if I was her personal secretary. Just because we lived in the same town didn't mean I had any special insights into her movements. The only time I knew what Idell was up to was when she had me chauffer her to the doctor's office.

But Mom made me call and ask her what everybody wanted to know. I listened to her answer, asked her if she was sure, said goodbye, then hung up the phone.

"Well?"

I looked around to find half-a-dozen relatives staring at me. "She says she's not coming," I told them. "She said she has no interest in seeing 'her Walter' in such a state. And she's tired."

People shrugged and went about their business. Mom looked at me like she was waiting for more, but there wasn't any more to say. Idell had said it all, and I couldn't say I disagreed with her.

"Well, that's our Idell," a cousin offered.

When I had moved in with Aunt Idell, she was in her seventies and her memory was as sharp and healthy as the rest of her body. Even though well past retirement age, Idell worked in her stores and oversaw everything until she finally had to give it up when she hit 85. She didn't sell though, and turned the day-to-day operations over to a man who had worked for her for years.

Idell and her husband never had any children. After she became my dad's guardian, she put all her motherly love into raising him. One of my most vivid childhood memories is watching my dad cry when Idell decided to move out to Long Beach and start her own appliance store. Jimmy had died the year before, a sudden heart attack. I was 3, but I remember the way my dad held his face in his hands while he cried. Idell patted him on the back and told him not to worry. "We'll see each like we always do," she said. "There's nothing to cry about." Turns out my dad's worries were valid and based on something rather than nothing.

•　　　•　　　•

Our family has lived in, or near, Crown City, California since the 1860s. Idell broke away in the early '70s when she decided she would have better luck with owning her own business out in Long Beach. Even though we have a lot of history here and most folks have hung around, we don't have yearly reunions or carry on about the past like Pamela's family. Whenever more than half-a-dozen of us get together and someone starts talking about the time so-and-so did such-and-such, it's not long before someone else jumps in with another version of events, and then the arguing starts.

Idell's version goes like this:

My father's great-great-grandparents left Galveston, Texas, on June 20, 1865. That was one day after General Granger, a member of the Union Army, stood on the balcony of Ashton Villa and announced that all the enslaved people were free. This news came more than two years after Abraham Lincoln had signed the Emancipation Proclamation, but with the Civil War going on and all those slave owners in no hurry to lose all that free labor, it took a while for the news to reach that tiny island in the Gulf of Mexico.

Our ancestor, Marcus, worked as a blacksmith on one of the larger plantations, and he wasted no time in getting away. He took the president's first name as his last name, packed up his wife and his two sons, and headed out the next day with every intention of going to the East Coast and getting on one of those boats to Africa. The story goes that they had been traveling for about a month before he realized they were headed in the wrong direction. His wife refused to turn around, so they kept going west and stopped when they ran into a range of mountains. His wife refused to go another step.

Not much is remembered about how they made a living, but whatever they did must have been enough. After a few years, Marcus had his own house and a bit of land too. Some people say that Marcus Abraham worked in the new citrus fields picking lemons along with the few other Blacks who lived in the area. Others say that he actually owned a small lemon grove himself. But he and his wife did fight a lot, and this is where the story gets confusing. One story goes that she stayed and gave birth three more times. Another version has her leaving—the husband and the sons—and going back to Galveston. This version is probably true because one of the older sons would talk about how, one day, his mother had … changed.

"We came home from pickin' and there was this other woman in the house, wearing my momma's clothes and sleeping in the bed with Daddy. When one of us got up the nerve to ask who she was and what happened to Momma, Daddy slapped us across the face and shout, 'That's your momma. Y'all lost your mind or something?'"

He said that he and his brother could tell that that wasn't their momma, but they got so afraid to say anything, they let it go.

"Momma wasn't that great anyway," he'd say. "At least this one could cook."

So, the new, or old, Mrs. Marcus Abraham gave birth to three more children, two boys and a girl, and then she died. Marcus followed her to the grave about six months later, and the children from his first wife took over raising their half-siblings. We don't know how long they were together, at least 10 Years, but in all that time Marcus never confessed to anyone the truth about the other woman.

After all the children were old enough to take care of themselves, the first set of sons began to start their own families. The second set of Abraham children stayed around, and one of them, Buster, got married to a young girl from a nearby town. That's when the big secret had to be acknowledged. This girl happened to be the niece of wife number two, which made the two of them not just cousins, but first cousins. The wedding was over and done with before the town could stop them. She lost two babies in two years, and everyone said it was because of their kinship.

But that didn't deter them. They kept trying, and after a while my dad's grandmother was born around 1888, and like everyone feared, she came out special. Her body grew all right, but her mind stayed a little girl her whole life. They named her Abbey, and because she was a girl in a woman's body, no man was willing to marry her—take advantage of her behind the barn after sundown, no problem— but to actually do right by her, that was a different thing altogether.

Abbey's parents were pretty good at catching any developments in time and then taking care of it, but after they did that twice, her mother said she couldn't stand it anymore.

"If the Good Lord is so set on this child having a baby, then I won't stand in His way no more." She said. A year or so after that, in 1913, my dad's mom was born. They named her Precious Abraham and everyone took a big sigh of relief when it looked like she had not inherited her mother's condition.

Precious Abraham was long, skinny, and as bald as an orange. The only thing on her that resembled her mother was her huge round eyes that popped out of her forehead like two ping-pong balls. Her parents were forever examining the other men in town looking for traits or similarities they could use to claim paternity. Every now and then an uncle or cousin would come by and say, "I believe that Travis Henry sho' has the same thin flat nose as our Precious." Then they'd look over at Abbey and wait for her to confess, or at least give a hint that they were on the right path. But she never said a word about any of it. She probably didn't even understand what they wanted from her.

After she gave birth, Abbey's mental state got worse. Before the baby she could do most things for herself and help around the house a bit. But after Precious was born, Abbey couldn't even dress herself anymore. Pretty soon she had to be spoon fed right alongside her own child. By the time Precious was five, she was doing things for her mother that the mother should have been doing for the child.

Precious kept on taking care of Abbey until she started school at about six years old. At about the same time, Butler and his wife surprised everyone and had Idell in 1923. Since Precious was older than her auntie, the care-giver roles were reversed again and all of a sudden, she found herself spending more time at home looking after both her mother and her auntie. School became something she had to work in after everything else was taken care of. Sometimes a cousin or neighbor would come by to help out and that's when Precious would take off—where to no one really knew for sure, but just when everybody started to worry about her, they would look up and see her strolling down the street back towards the house.

"Where you been?" they would ask.

"No where you need to know about," was the only answer she gave.

So that's how things went in the Abraham house for about ten years. Idell was old enough to look after herself by then, and Abbey was so far gone there was nothing more to do except wait. Precious had managed to squeeze in enough schooling to get a high school diploma and was taking odd jobs around town. But then one night, Precious announced she was moving away.

Idell panicked. Her mother and father were needing more care and looking after, and the Depression had made times tough for everybody. Idell used to be able to rely on family for help, but by then, most were either too busy or had stopped offering help. Idell tried to talk Precious out of leaving. She promised she would do more around the house and that Precious could come and go as much as she liked. As long as she came back.

"I do that already," Precious told her.

"But what about your momma?" Idell asked.

Precious looked over at Abbey. She was still sitting up in the same chair they had put her in that morning. Her mouth hung open and a steady stream of drool soaked into the big towel they laid across her chest. Abbey hadn't said a word in over seven years.

"I've been doing for others all my life, and now I'm about ready to start doing for myself."

Idell repeated her earlier question.

"Don't worry," Precious assured her. "I'll see she's taken care of before I leave."

Idell relaxed a little bit, then thought of something else. "But what about momma and daddy? Are you gonna tell them?"

"I'll leave them a letter. You can read it to them after I'm gone."

Two nights later, Abbey died in her sleep. When Idell went to tell Precious, she found her standing in front of the going-away mirror adjusting her hat.

"Precious, your momma is dead."

Precious didn't answer. She took a long sharp hat pin and stabbed it through the band and into the thick ball of hair underneath. She continued adjusting her hat, not bothering to look at her auntie.

"I left a note for the others on the kitchen table. You can read it to them later."

Their eyes finally met in the mirror, and for a few seconds neither spoke. Idell was afraid of the thoughts running through her mind, and the cold look in Precious' eyes was anything but reassuring.

The sound of movement from the back of the house told them that their folks were up. Precious bent down and picked up her suitcase and told Idell she would send money whenever she could and turned to leave.

Idell stared at her back as she walked the few steps to the front door. Precious had almost closed the front door behind her when Idell finally found her voice.

"I know what you did, Precious."

Precious didn't turn. "Go to your folks, Idell. They need you." She closed the door behind her, and Idell did as she was told. She never did read that letter. The first few days she was so mad at her niece she didn't want any reminder of her. Hate turned to fear when Idell contemplated what Precious may have written. A confession? An apology? Either way made no difference to Idell, so she burned the letter in the stove the day after Abbey's funeral. Her parents asked about their granddaughter once or twice, but soon settled into the fact that she had left, and for good this time.

After about a year, Idell got a letter from Precious. This one she read. Precious was in a little city called Long Beach. She wrote how a lot of people had left the city after the earthquake so there were lots of jobs. Precious worked as a maid in one of the bigger, and still standing, hotels called The Breakers. She said it was like cleaning up after her momma, except she got paid for it. After Idell read the letter to her parents, they smiled and seemed glad that their granddaughter was finally happy.

In Crown City, Idell had nothing else to do but stay at home, help her folks, and work odd jobs. Her daddy was a pretty good provider and taught Idell how to plan and save. They weren't rich, but Idell doesn't remember ever going without.

When she was almost 20, both her parents died, one from a stroke, the other a broken heart. Precious had been gone about 8 years. She wrote regularly at first, but after the first few years, the letters hardly came. But all that was about to change.

After World War II started, Idell got another letter from Precious letting her know that all the hotel jobs had dried up with everyone going off to fight the Germans and the Japanese. For the first time, she asked Idell to send her some money. But instead of that, Idell wrote back to tell her to come on home; oranges and lemons still needed picking, and with all the young men gone there was plenty of work for the women.

Precious never got that letter. It came back to Idell about two months after she mailed it. Idell didn't have time to give it much thought though. Later that morning, she was out sweeping the front porch and looked up to see her niece walking down the road, headed straight for the house. Just like before, but not quite.

Along with her clothes, some small souvenirs for Idell, and a five-cent bag of salt-water taffy for the cousins, Precious brought home a baby boy. For the first half hour Precious talked about everything but the baby, kept moving it from one arm to the other like a sack of groceries. After she talked all about Long Beach and how nice and fancy it was, the hotels and everything else that baby—my daddy—started to holler.

Idell, who didn't know what else to say, asked, "What's that?" Precious didn't answer her, so she asked the next question. "Is it yours?"

"What kinda question is that Idell? Why would I be carrying this child if it wasn't mine?"

"Where the daddy at?"

"Oh, Jesus Idell, don't you know nothing? Don't you all get the newspapers down here?"

"Why would your baby be in the papers?"

Precious started talking to Idell like she was speaking to a three-year-old. "Listen, all the men had to go overseas to fight those Japs, Idell."

"All the men? Even the Coloreds?"

"Yes, the Coloreds, too. And that's where he is."

"Fighting those Japs? When will he be back?"

"They can't say. That's what they call top-secret information."

"Well, can you tell me his name at least?"

"His name is Walter. Walter Roberts."

"Not the daddy's name. What's the name of your baby, Precious."

Precious looked at Idell, "They names is the same. Walter Roberts."

After about a week, Idell decided that Walter Roberts, Jr. was the fussiest baby she had ever known. He screamed for his momma's tit every hour, and in between that time he screamed for no reason she could figure out. He only stopped when he slept, which was never longer than forty-five minutes. At six months Precious cut him off her breast and started feeding him mashed potatoes and rice. Idell tried to warn her that it was too soon, but Precious wasn't listening.

"What do you know about babies, Idell?" Precious asked her.

"I know Mrs. Shifton still has her baby sucking off her, and he's walking."

"And have you seen her? That baby and the five she had before done sucked all the life out of her. No wonder her men keep running off."

Idell picked up her grandnephew and wiped his face. "Maybe that last one didn't run off, Precious. Maybe he off doing top-secret army work, too."

"Shut-up, Idell. You don't know what you're talking about." Precious got up and looked at herself in the going-away mirror, still hanging in the hallway by the front door. It was the mirror you checked yourself in right before leaving the house. "Besides," she said, looking herself over, "I've got to think about getting a job and getting back out there."

Idell shifted Walter to her other shoulder. "Mrs. Johnson gets a check every month from the Navy 'cause of her husband being off on that ship. When you gonna start getting money, Precious?"

"I told you that it's different with my man. What he's doing is special and secret. Mr. Johnson is probably just peeling potatoes and mopping floors."

Idell didn't answer her. She had begun to suspect that her niece was making up stories about the top-secret life of Sergeant Walter Roberts. And besides, despite his constant fussiness, she was getting attached to Little Walter, and the idea of his momma spending more time out of the house than in it appealed to her. She moved Walter to her other shoulder and patted his back.

"I heard that they was getting ready to hire out at Redball again. Mr. Johnson always liked you. I'm sure he'll take you back."

Picking oranges wasn't the kind of work Precious had in mind. She unbuttoned her dress to look at herself. "You know I used to watch those white ladies doing all sorts of exercises with their arms and legs." She laughed. "They looked like they were getting ready to fly somewhere."

Precious lifted her arms up until she looked like the Cross and began whirling her arms around. She turned her head to Idell.

"They told me this one was good for the chest and arms."

"You don't need to do that, Precious. After two weeks of picking, your arms and chest will be strong enough."

Precious kept on. She had every intention of going to see Mr. Johnson, but not about picking fruit.

Even though Precious couldn't tell a typewriter from an adding machine, she wiggled her way into a secretary type job at the Redball Office. In between all the pretend filing and typing, she poured all her energy into courting and catching Mr. Johnson. Whatever happened to Walter Roberts, Sr. no one ever knew. Precious stopped mentioning him and his top-secret work, and Idell stopped asking. And then Mr. Johnson was showing up at the house with baskets of oranges and bouquets of flowers. Precious may not have been any good at typing or filing, but she sure could flirt and make a man want her, which Mr. Johnson did after about three months. Precious was smart this time and insisted upon marriage.

Mrs. Precious Johnson came back to the house to get her clothes and hats and shoes and that's all. She pleaded with Idell to look after Walter for a few weeks.

"Just until Xavier and I can get to know each other." She pleaded. "We're newlyweds, Idell. How do you expect us to have a honeymoon with a baby around?"

A few weeks turned into a few months, and then months turned into years. Precious would get her son and keep him for a week or two, but she always had an excuse for delivering him back into Idell's arms. Idell stopped fussing with her about it. She suspected Precious was mistreating the boy, and Idell couldn't stand the thought of that. Whenever Precious fetched him, he had a full belly and clean clothes. When he came back, he was always starved, dirty, and traumatized.

After Walter's second birthday, he and Idell were a solid pair and had settled into a nice routine. He was walking, talking, playing, and smiling. Next door to Idell, the Bailey family had a whole pack of kids for him to play with. The older ones would look after Little Walter while Idell was working or out running errands. At home they had the house to themselves, food on the table, good neighbors willing to lend a hand, and even had money to spare for going to the movies, an ice cream soda now and then, and a big fat peppermint stick to suck on during church on Sundays. At four years old, my dad was one fat, happy Black kid. Probably the happiest in his life, I suspect.

.             .             .

Even though the house was still full of guests, I told Mom I needed to lie down before Pamela and Jackson arrived. She quizzed me again about Idell, then let me go when it was clear I wasn't holding out on her, which I wasn't.

On my way back to the bedroom, I peeked in on my father. He was alone, lying peacefully on his side, eyes closed. Someone had left a half-empty Styrofoam cup of coffee on his nightstand and a crumpled-up napkin. I threw it all away and saw the coffee ring it made on his temperature chart. I smoothed out the sheets over his body and adjusted his pillow. Before leaving, I felt his forehead. It was pretty cool. I felt his cheek, too. Still smooth.

# Chapter 14

Jackson jumping on my bed woke me up. I opened my eyes to see my son's face beaming down at me.

"Hi Daddy. You asleep?"

"I was." I scrambled to sit up and gave him a hug. As soon as I released him, he launched into a long and detailed recap of the events of the last two days. According to him, the memorial was boring, his Grandpa BJ cried, Grandma Liz made the best chocolate cake, and his cousin Greg got some really cool monster truck Hot Wheels for his birthday.

"He says I can play with them when we come over to his house. When are we going to his house, Dad?"

I liked watching his little mouth moving as he talked, cheeks puffing in and out. He was talking fast, like he was afraid he'd forget something.

"I don't know, Jackson. They live a long way away."

"This is a long way away," he said.

"Not as long as where Aunt Paula and Uncle Mark live. We have to fly to get to their house." I was up, tucking my shirt back in and trying to look presentable again.

He sighed. "I wish we could have used an airplane here. Mom had to drive a loooong time."

I looked down at him and felt an ounce of guilt for him having to endure the long car ride. Plus, with no other kids in the neighborhood and Cholé all into Barbies, he'd be bored out of his little mind within the hour.

"Well, we should be back home in a day or two," I said. "Hey, how would you like your Grandpa Walt to come live with us?"

His eyes grew wide. "But Mommy says he's real sick. That's why we came to see him."

"He is sick," I told him, "but I want to bring him to our house so we can take good care of him."

Jackson sat on the bedside, his little feet swung back and forth. He still had on his dress shirt and pants from the memorial, but the clip-on tie was gone. He stopped moving his feet.

"Can't he go to where Grandma Rose was at? It was pretty there."

My own son was against me. Before I could answer him, Pamela came through the door. She still had on the dress she wore to the memorial, absent the high heels and hose.

"There you are," she said to both of us.

Jackson blurted out, "Dad says Grandpa Walt is coming to live with us. Is he Mom? Where's he gonna sleep?"

Pamela snapped her head in my direction. "Why'd you tell him that," she said, barely moving her lips.

"I just asked him his opinion." That sounded lame, even to me.

She shook her head, kneeled to be face to face with Jackson and told him that I had made a mistake.

"Grandpa Walt is staying here with Grandma, Honey. Daddy made a mistake, OK? So don't say anything to Grandma or Uncle Bobby about what he said, all right?" She lifted him in her arms and stood up. "John, tell your son you made a mistake."

I did as she told me, which satisfied him. To him, the subject was closed. She pecked him on the cheek, set him down and told him to go tell everyone that Mommy and Daddy had to talk.

"Have you lost your mind, John?" she said as soon as our son left. "I just talked with your mother, and she says that Walter is staying here. Period. What's gotten in to you telling him those things? You're going to confuse him."

"Confuse him about what? A son wanting to care for his sick father? What's confusing about that?"

"It's confusing because he hears one thing from everybody else and something different from you."

"Well, I know what he's been hearing from you. He thinks my dad should go to Peaceful Horizons."

"He said that?" She smiled.

"It's not funny, and I don't appreciate my son being brain-washed against me."

She kept smiling. "He wasn't brain-washed. He's smart."

I snapped. For the last three days, everyone who is supposed to love me has done nothing but tell me how stupid I was acting. And being told that my own five-year-old son was my intellectual superior was too much.

"Why is everybody fighting me on this? He's my dad, and I deserve this. He's been with Bobby and Mom all these years, why can't I get my chance now?" At a time when I needed to sound mature and put together, I came off like a second grader hollering over missing his turn at kickball.

Pamela's mood changed, to pity, which I didn't need either. "John, I know you think—"

"No, you don't because you've never asked me what I think. You and Mom and Bobby have just told me how stupid I am."

She took a small step towards me. "John, calm down. I'm sorry. I never meant to call you stupid. But we need to talk about this later. Not now."

"Did you see him? We may not have a later, Pamela." The tears that sprang to my eyes surprised me. She looked a bit surprised, too.

She studied my face before responding. "I really don't know what to say to you, John," she offered after a decent pause. "What you're wanting right now is pretty impossible. I—we—don't understand how you can't see that."

"It's not impossible. Your dad did it."

After a pause, she asked, "What's going on?" The question in her words matched the one on her face.

"I told you. You and everybody else are ganging up against me."

She huffed. "Oh, John. Don't be so—"

"Stupid?" I finished her thought, crossed my arms and looked back at her. I was mad and hurt. "You know why I keep thinking about Janet and the twins? Because all the time we were together, hanging out and having fun, they never called me stupid."

Her eyes narrowed, and any pity she may have had vanished. I watched her face change from sorrow to astonishment, and then rage. She stood before me, her house-shoe clad feet firmly anchored to the floor, hands clenched by her side. I'd be lying if I said I wasn't a little intimidated. Bringing Janet into the equation had been dumber than dumb.

"There is no way I'm getting into this anymore. The decision has been made, and I am not going against your mother's wishes." She turned to leave, but stopped at the door. "If you still want to do this, you're on your own." Glancing at me over her shoulder she added, "But maybe you can get Janet to help you. Or one of your other … ."

That last part choked out of her along with a cracked sob. Before I could respond, she walked out and closed the door. It didn't make a sound; a stark contrast to the sound my heart made slamming against my chest.

There were a lot of things I could have done after my wife left the room. A lot of really smart things. Like go after her, apologize and beg for forgiveness. I could have also thrown another apology at Mom and Bobby and promised to do whatever they wanted me to do. With Dad, I could have let myself forgive him, been around when he really needed me, and made our last days together pretty special. I'd bring my family down to visit a lot more so I could give him a good shave. Jackson would see me as a loving and kind son. My wife would see that too, and maybe her suspicions about me would vanish, and I would never give her a reason to doubt me again.

All that would have been really nice. But I didn't do any of it, and the only explanation I have to offer is that Pamela and Mom and Bobby were right all along. I am stupid.

When I turned the corner and saw the lights on, nostalgia overtook me. Suddenly I was fifteen years old again, going over to my best friends' house, escaping the loneliness and hostility of my own home.

I knocked and waited. Jamal answered the door.

"John? Wow. Jeff and I were just talking about going over to see you all tomorrow after the store closed." He stepped to the side. "Come on in."

I walked in, and he stepped onto the porch and looked down the street before closing the door. "You alone?"

I nodded, not trusting my voice yet. He waited for more, but when nothing came, he ushered me into the living room. The first thing I noticed was how nothing had changed: same furniture, same carpet, same pictures on the wall, and the same photos on the bookshelves. The only additions were portraits of the twins in their cap and gowns. One set from high school, another from college. Their diplomas were hung there as well. No adult pictures of Janet though. Just the same ones from all those years ago, plus her debutante ball portrait. Minus Eric Baker.

Jamal invited me to sit down, after he yelled for his brother. Jeff emerged from the kitchen wearing what I recognized as one of his mother's old aprons. He was holding a pair of tongs.

"Well, look what the cat dragged in!" His smile was big and genuine. "Just in time for dinner." He winked. "Like always."

Jamal sat down opposite me in what used to be his father's chair. He leaned forward.

"How's your dad doing, John? We heard from the Levi's he's in pretty bad shape."

Jeff sprang forward. "Jamal, don't be so insensitive." He turned to me. "John, just know that everyone in the neighborhood is praying for your dad."

"I was just saying what we heard, Jeff. John's not stupid. He knew what I meant."

Jeff started to reply, but then stopped, lifted his nose and sniffed the air. "Oh, heck. The chicken." He turned and scurried towards the kitchen. "See what you always make me do?"

Jeff disappeared through the kitchen door, leaving me alone with Jamal, who stared at Jeff's wake, shaking his head.

I swallowed hard and tried to wrap my brain around what I was witnessing. Jeff and Jamal, the mighty, no bullshit Moore twins, had mutated into Lucy and Ricky Ricardo.

Jamal said he was sorry about his brother and offered me a beer. I accepted, and he stood up and told me to follow him.

"I have to keep it out in the garage. Jeff won't stand it in the house."

The garage was the one aspect of the house that had changed. It looked like a new concrete floor had been put in, and the walls were finished in drywall with wood cabinets attached. All the tools were arranged on wall hooks or in tool boxes. On one side, the counter was stacked with old PC towers, keyboards and printers. I wondered which one of them had taken up computer repair. It was Jamal. He told me he liked to tinker on the old PCs, get them running and upgrade them.

"I donate them to schools or nursing homes and such. I built Janet's last computer." He took a sip of his beer and raised his eyebrows. "You seen it?"

I choked on the swallow in my throat and shook my head no in between coughs. "What did she tell you? I only saw her that one time. First time in almost twenty years."

He laughed. "I know, man. Just messing with you."

Ha, ha, I thought.

"Hey, how old is that son of yours?" he said. "I could set him up with a starter system. Nothing too fancy; just enough memory to play games or doodle. Keep him off the internet though. Too much shit out there."

A picture of a little computer in my soon to be single apartment flashed in front of me. When Jackson came over during court approved visitation, he could play on it.

"Let me think about it," I told him.

He finished off his beer and grabbed another from the fridge. "So you're all settled down now. Wife. Kid. House. And a pretty good job from what I hear."

His use of the present tense comforted me. "Yep." I answered. He waited for more, but I didn't want to talk about my so-called settled life. "I wanted to ask you about getting some help for my dad."

"What kind of help? Magnolia Gardens usually takes care of all that stuff."

He knew everything. "No. Not about that. I want to take care of my dad myself. At my house." After everything Pamela had told me, and the sense she made, I was still being stubborn. But it was pretty much a moot point by then, I just didn't know it.

He glanced at me with the same look of pity Pamela had.

"Look John, I know how you feel, but take if from a son who just went through all of that. Jeff and my dad insisted that Mom stay here, and it turned into one big nightmare. No nurse was ever good enough, and the paramedics threatened to stop coming out if we didn't get her in a nursing home. And the one nurse that was worth a damn ran off with Dad after Mom died. If I could do it all over again, I'd put her in Magnolia, like your mom is planning to do." He gave my shoulder a reassuring squeeze. "Try to let it go, man. Trust me."

"You mean like I trusted you all those years ago?" One thing had absolutely nothing to do with the other, but I really hadn't gone over there to talk about my dad.

He took a deep breath. "Things didn't go right back then. For none of us."

"What do you mean 'us'? Who kicked you out of your house?"

He took a long swallow. "I wish it had been me." He tossed his empty beer can into the trash, but didn't get another one. I watched him walk over to his workbench and sit down on the stool; he put one foot up on the first rung, the other on the cement floor. "John Roberts, you getting out of this place was the best thing that could have happened to you. If you had stayed here, you'd be stuck with … ."

"Stuck with who? Janet? That's what I wanted."

"Yeah, we knew that's what you wanted. Look, man, I was really pissed at you. I mean you knocked-up my sister. What was I supposed to do?"

I took a step towards him. "Yeah, but you knew me. I was your friend. Your best friend. You should have known it was more than just sex between us."

He held up his hands like a boxer blocking a right jab. "Hey man, I get it. But she's still my sister, all right?"

"I loved her."

He recoiled and a look of disgust crossed his face. "So? That was almost two decades ago. You turned out OK. What do you want now? An apology? For what? An older brother looking out for his kid sister?"

"I was pissed as hell that no one would listen to us. Janet loved me, too, you know."

A short and loud laugh erupted past his lips. "Janet loved you? You don't know shit, man." He shook his head. "I hate to admit this about my own sister, but she played you, just like all of us. She jerked you around, then Mom, then Dad, and now she tries that shit on me. Why do you think she's waiting tables?"

I didn't know, but it was a question that had been on my mind.

"Because she can't be trusted to work at the stores," he said. "She screws up every responsibility we give her. Hell, the only job I would let her do now comes with a bucket and a mop but how would that look. Dad tried to get her to stay in college; he paid for everything, but would she take advantage of it? Mom finally convinced him to just let her be. She said Janet had to 'find her own way,' whatever the hell that meant."

After a pause, he continued. "Janet never appreciated how we all loved her and only wanted the best for her. Didn't appreciate it then and still doesn't. And our mom? She loved Janet to death." Our eyes met. "And I mean that literally."

Jamal was truly dismayed with his little sister's lifestyle choices, but he was just like Bobby—loyal to papa bear all the way. I knew from our talks that Janet hated the pharmaceutical business, her brother's bullying, and her dad's strict rules. But she knew how to get around all of it and not let them stop her from doing what she really wanted to do. Like sneaking around with me, or waiting tables for a living. She didn't need them.

"Janet and I used to talk about our families." I said, smiling at the memory. "That's one thing we had in common. She always told me about—"

"I don't want to hear about it. All right?" He stood up so fast the stool tipped over.

"Jamal, I just need you to understand how it was," I said. "I don't know why it's so important to me, but it is. It always has been."

I knew my obsession over this was not the healthiest way to live, but he looked at me that night like I had just told him I had a terminal cancer with only weeks to live. The sympathy in his eyes was something I had never seen before.

"Look, John," he said, "if you say you loved her, I believe you. Hell, you might even think yourself still in love with her for all I know. But you'll have to believe me when I tell you this: Janet never loved you back."

"You don't know that," I said.

He looked at the house before answering. Jeff was still inside, tending to his fried chicken. "My sister is incapable of loving anyone. Except herself." He got close to me and lowered his voice before continuing. "And deep down, you knew that too, didn't you? You're mad because I didn't stand up for you? What about Janet?" He answered his own question. "She was quiet as the grave about you, man. No hollering how she loved you and shit. After the baby was gone, she went on as if nothing happened."

He started towards the house but I had more to say. "You didn't understand her back then; none of you did. She hated that about all of you."

He stopped. "What do you mean 'back then'? She acts exactly the same way she did when she was fourteen. The only thing that's changed is the time. We grew up; she didn't."

"I don't know what happened after I left—"

"Everything happened, but nothing changed. I can give you the name of half a dozen boys Janet claimed she 'loved.' I'm sorry if you thought you were different, but you weren't. There was no difference, man. No difference."

He gave me one more look, but turned away abruptly after I opened my mouth to speak.

"Go home, John Roberts. Your family needs you." he said right before disappearing through the screen door. I faintly heard Jeff asking about me, and then Jamal telling him I had to leave. I left through the back gate.

# Chapter 15

I took the long way back to the house, which meant going around the block in the opposite direction and through the same alleys and streets Janet and I used to walk. It was late, dark, and cold. I shoved my hands inside my pants pockets and walked with my head down. No one at home had noticed when I snuck through the kitchen and out the back door, but I was sure my absence had been discovered. My phone was still on the dresser in my old room. They'd all be mad at me, maybe not Jackson. He would be scared and worried, though. But Pamela would know how to calm him. She always did.

My mind couldn't stay on one train of thought long enough for me to make sense of anything. Jeff, Jamal, Janet, Pamela, Dad, Mom, Bobby, even Aunt Idell and Kim, ricocheted within the synapses of my brain like an out-of-control pinball. I got clarity on nothing, so I kept on walking, hoping that a message of enlightenment and guidance would come to me on the cold and dark streets of Crown City.

It didn't, and after a half hour I turned around and headed home. The only thing left to do was face it all and hope the aftermath wasn't too bad. I'd insist on joint custody. Probably wouldn't get it, but I'd try, anyway.

I was far from having any idea of how to fix the mess I had made of my life, but one thing about me began to feel a little better. That chip on my shoulder over the so-call injustices of my youth fell off somewhere between Spring Street and Lake Ave. Mom had asked me a good question the other night. What did I want?

After witnessing the twins in action, being friends with them like the old days was just plain laughable. And Janet? In my version of Janet's life post-John Roberts, she had fallen apart after our force separation, a real train wreck, and longing for me day in and day out. Just like I had. That's the real reason why I wanted to talk to her. Jamal, Bobby, and Natalyn were not the only ones to tell me about Janet's affairs after I left, but I needed to hear it from her. But then what?

I turned the final corner and groaned when I saw an extra car in front of the house. Just what I needed: more witnesses to my downfall. Who the hell was still there? All the lights were on, but the living room looked empty through the front window. I walked up the front steps, took a deep breath, grabbed the doorknob, turned it, and pushed the door open.

The front room was empty. It looked like the aftermath of a cocktail party with empty plates, glasses, and coffee cups scattered about. One cup, on the small coffee table, must have still had hot coffee in it because I thought I saw a thin line of steam floating up and towards the ceiling. The only sound I could make out was the background chatter and music of a Disney cartoon playing in the den, so I knew where the kids were. I came all the way in and quietly closed the door. My brain told my feet to walk, but they stayed still. I figured my mind was still tripping, so I closed my eyes, leaned back against the door, and took a deep breath. Then a shiver ran through me, and I felt like a man who had just come in from the snow.

I kept my eyes closed and took another deep breath and saw that little girl from my dream standing in front of me. She didn't have any apples, and she looked really sad. I panicked and looked around hoping to see an apple I could give to her to make her happy again, but the room was too smoky to see anything. I coughed. She lifted her open hands to me, wanting me to give her something, but I could only shake my head no, I didn't have anything to give her. A second later she was gone.

When I opened my eyes, I saw my wife watching me. She stood very still; like a statue. A statue with tears running down its face.

# Chapter 16

He aspirated, followed by asphyxiation. That's when a semi-comatose patient throws up, tries to swallow, and ends up choking on it instead. His doctor told us it was one of the risks associated with his condition. No one did anything wrong, and he had received the best care possible.

The extra car belonged to the nurse on call. Most of the guests had left, and everyone else was in the living room when my mom heard him in distress, my absence was still undiscovered. When she entered his room, Dad was coughing and hacking his brains out. She tried to get his suction thing going, but he was just too agitated. She yelled for Bobby who came to help, but he was too freaked out. Pamela found the phone number on the fridge and called the nursing service. A nurse named Sandy arrived twenty minutes later. Dad had grown still by then. She assessed him and gave the grim news.

"I'm sorry," she said. But they called an ambulance anyway, and the paramedics arrived just to pronounce him dead. They took their report, made sure Mom was all right, checked Bobby's blood pressure, and left. Sandy had to stay around and complete a shit load of paperwork, plus she wanted to be there when the mortuary driver came. Very considerate, I thought. Sometime when all that had been going on, Pamela went to my room to get me. When she saw I wasn't there, she re-closed my door and told my mom I was still asleep.

"Let him sleep. He's going to need his strength." Mom was either too tired or too distressed to put up an argument. Or maybe she knew I was gone, since my bedroom was the closest to Dad's, and I should have been the first to hear him. If I had been there.

Bobby was a wreck. Natalyn tried her best to console him, but it was no use. The nurse ended up slipping him something to calm him down, which everyone was grateful for. The kids had fallen asleep in front of the TV, and that's where they had stayed. They would find out in the morning that their grandfather was gone. If Pamela had thought my behavior at the front door strange, she kept quiet about it.

"He's gone," was all she told me.

•          •          •

The funeral was the following week. Pamela stayed around to help, which everyone appreciated. Those plans and arrangements Bobby had told me about were pretty complete. Dad had arranged and prepaid for the burial and even picked out his coffin. Mom had a few little details to decide on, and she turned those over to Bobby and me. She was like a zombie, and if it hadn't been for Pamela encouraging her to eat and take care of herself, we may have had two funerals that week.

Idell came down the very next day. She stayed at the house and slept in dad's hospital bed. None of us bothered to protest or try to change her mind. You just didn't do that with Aunt Idell. On the outside she maintained her composure. Everyone kept saying how strong and together she was, but I wished she would let it all out.

No one said much to me. I would press myself into a corner and watch as family and friends came and went, offering their condolences and leaving a casserole, a cake, or a bucket of fried chicken. I got out of the house as much as I could by taking Jackson, and sometimes Cholé, to the park or McDonald's. People seemed to appreciate that saying the kids needed a break. I also served as the airport chauffer, driving back and forth about three times that week.

I estimated over a hundred people came out for his service, and about two-thirds of them came by the house afterwards. Tyrone, Susie, and Ted came. Matt and Lisa sent a huge potted plant that looked like something straight out of the rain forest.

At the house, I stayed in my corner for as long as I could, but an hour into it I started to suffocate and had to get out. The back yard was set up with tables and chairs, but only the smokers in the family were out there. The day was overcast, with a slight chill in the air. When the cousins and friends saw me come out, they stopped talking. Each looked up at me with a forced smile that did nothing to hide the pity in their eyes.

"How ya' doing, John?"

I couldn't answer them, just like I couldn't answer the other fifty people who had already asked me that. Instead, I bummed a cigarette and escaped into the garage.

My first inhale didn't go down so well. It hurt like hell, but I didn't stop. I was never a smoker, just a cigarette every now and then. I quit for good when I started selling real estate. My dad smoked occasionally. One pack would last him almost a month.

The stories Aunt Idell had told me were mostly to try to get me to feel some sympathy towards my dad; all that history about how his mother hardly did any mothering, and how he never knew his real father. And then the big screw-up when Precious finally came back for him. For good.

Precious' husband died and his grown kids, who had been MIA since forever, showed up before the dirt had time to settle around the coffin and proceeded to take everything he owned. They even took Precious' wedding band, claiming that their daddy still owed money, and it should go back to the jeweler.

Precious slinked back to the old house the exact same way she had left it all those years ago: broke and alone. By that time, Idell was treating little Walter as her own, and Precious' idea to take him back didn't sit so well with her. Idell tried to talk her niece into letting Walter stay with her, but Precious wasn't having it. No, no, and no, were her only answers.

A week later, Precious and Walter Roberts Jr. vanished. Idell never got any details about exactly where she planned on going, and it wasn't until later that she found out Precious had run off with a man who worked in the groves at Red Ball—a married man. People round Red Ball said he talked a lot about moving up to Oregon and working in a lumber mill. He left his kids behind; Precious took hers.

Unlike the last time, Precious never wrote to say where she was or how she was making a living. After about a year of waiting and wondering, Idell tried to file the memory or her grandnephew away and get on with her life. Since graduating, she worked in the appliance department of Montgomery Wards. That's where she met Jimmy Brooks, the man who would later become her husband, then her business partner. But she never could get her nephew out of her mind. She would tell me that sometimes at night, she could hear little Walter calling for her. "Right after I married Jimmy, I told him I had to go up to Oregon and look for my Walter." And that's just what she did.

The only clues Idell knew to locate her nephew were the ones she got from that man's children. Their father had written them, and they gave Idell his return address. She took a train up to Portland, then a taxi to the address on the envelope. It was a boarding house, and the landlord informed her that yes, Precious, a man, and a little boy lived there, but they left a few months ago.

"That boy of hers wouldn't shut-up for nothing," he said. "I ain't never seen a kid scream so loud and for so long." He took a short, cautious step towards Idell. "There was something definitely not right about them."

"What about the man?"

"Oh him. He ran off with the wife of the man in number three. Precious and that boy took off a few weeks after that. She owes me $7.50."

Idell paid the man, hoping he would provide more details. "Can you tell me which way she went at least?"

He counted the money and shook his head no. "The bug-eyed bitch snuck out in the middle of night. Can't say I missed that hollering boy either."

Idell made her way back to the street. The ground was wet from the recent rains, and there were no paved walkways or paths. Her shoes got covered in mud and while wiping them clean on the grass, a young woman appeared at her side. She was short and thin with dark, ashy arms that stuck out of her oversized and shabby dress like twigs. The mass of hair on top of her head resembled an unkept bird's nest. "I heard you asking about Precious and her boy," she whispered to Idell.

Idell told the lady who she was, and that she was worried about her nephew. "Was he all right the last time you seen him?"

"Well, he wasn't crying. I can tell you that much."

Idell doubted she knew more, but asked anyway.

The young lady looked Idell over while mumbling on about how hard a time Precious had with that bastard, and the last thing she wanted was to send another tormentor after her. She looked closely at Idell and probably recognized a bit of Precious in her expression. "You say you kin, huh?"

"Her auntie."

This seemed to satisfy the young woman. "Well, I can't say for sure, but she mentioned something about looking for work in a hotel or something. Talked about how she did that kinda work in California."

"Do you know which ones?" Idell asked her.

"Most likely the Seward, downtown. It's the biggest one and they hire Coloreds."

The hiring manager at the Seward Hotel remembered a pretty Colored girl and her boy, but he turned her away. Idell spent the next two days wandering from hotel to hotel, from boarding house to boarding house, and towards the end of her search, the hospitals. On the day before she was supposed to leave, she stopped by the county jail. After she told them who she was and who she was looking for, the desk sergeant looked her over. "Your niece," he said, "did she have really big eyes?"

Precious' body had been buried two weeks earlier in an unmarked grave. The coroner had a picture which Idell identified. "If it wasn't for those eyes, she'd look like any other molested and beat up Negro girl." She paid them $10 to place a maker on the grave, collected Precious's effects, but declined to visit the gravesite. "Where's my nephew?" she asked them.

Idell brought a frightened and traumatized Walter home with her. She said it took them a whole year to get him set right. He couldn't be left alone at night and refused to go to school. "I stopped working for months to stay home with him," she told me. "Jimmy and I poured all we had into that boy. We thought since he was so young, that he would eventually forget everything that happened up there. But he never did. Just when we thought he was over it all, he'd bring it up again."

The Portland Police had given Idell everything they collected from Precious, and among her clothes and Walter's things she found a bundle of letters and documents. There were pictures and postcards from Long Beach, all of Idell's letters, and Walter's birth certificate from St. Mary Hospital in Long Beach. The father was listed as "Unknown."

•　　　•　　　•

Pamela came into the garage as I was finishing the cigarette. My chest and lungs burned, but the heat felt good.

"There you are," she said. She stepped into the dark garage and closed the door behind her. Sunlight filtered in through the dirty window panes on the door. The light streamed in and made a four-square pattern on the concrete floor. The garage was damp and cool. The quiet hum of the freezer played in the background. Pamela folded her arms to warm herself, stepped to the side and leaned against the dryer. I didn't move from my spot next to the washer.

If I had kept my suit coat on, I would have offered it to her. Instead I just said, "It's cold in here."

She nodded and looked around. "A lot of memories in here, too." Pamela looked at me, hesitated, and then asked, "When did you start smoking again?"

"I haven't. I just felt like … ." I shrugged.

She nodded. And then we were silent again.

I followed her gaze to my old bike and skateboards. We had talked last Christmas about when would be a good time to get Jackson's first real bike and decided that he could wait one more year. My childhood Schwinn was too big for him and probably would be until he was at least ten. That bike had been a present for my twelfth birthday. Taking it back home to Long Beach and restoring it in my own garage really appealed to me. For the last few days, my thoughts had a distinct domestic edge to them. No more was I figuring out how to get away for a few hours, or stay out late. There would be no more late mee-tings.

Pamela straightened up and faced me. "Look, John," she began. "I've been thinking about this a lot, and there is no other way to say it. I know you may think now is the worst time, and I'm sorry about that, but … ."

I held my breath and waited. She waited too, maybe hoping I would finish for her. But after a half a minute of mutual silence, she continued. She took a deep breath.

"I don't want you to come back to the house. Not for a while, at least."

I heard her and nodded my head slowly. Not in agreement, but in understanding. Hell, if I was married to me, I wouldn't want me back in the house either. But it still hurt. I had been hoping and praying for a reprieve, a pass, or forgiveness.

I choked out an okay. "For how long?" I added.

"I can't answer that. It depends."

A bit of hope sparked. I stood to face her, looking her straight in the eyes. "Depends on what? Tell me, please. Whatever you want—"

"It may be too late for that, John."

"Please, Pamela, I'm sorry. Can't you—"

She held up a hand to stop me. "I know where you were that night, John. I know. I don't understand why, but I know."

Did she mean a week ago with Kim? Or was she talking about the night my father passed away? One was as bad as the other, so I was screwed either way. All I could do was lower my head and apologize.

She stayed quiet, waiting for more. "Is that all you have to say?" she asked after my too long silence. When nothing came, she opened the door. "I'm sorry too," she whispered. After the garage door closed behind her, I felt that coldness pass through me again. I shoved my hands in my pants' pocket, felt the change and pulled out a few coins.

Two Minnesotas.

# Chapter 17

Pamela and Jackson drove back to Long Beach without me. No one asked what was up, so I figured they understood the situation. I also found out that she had been referring to the night my dad died when we talked in the garage. The Moores stopped by sometime during the week between my dad's death and the funeral. Jeff told them I had gone over that night for comfort and prayer, but who would believe that? There must have been an uncomfortable shift in the air because Janet felt the need to add that she hadn't been at the house when I was there. Which I'm sure made it worse since it looked like she was speaking up for me. Only guilty people need that.

Idell relayed the story to me after I moved back into her place.

She sat on the sofa opposite me as she described who said what and how everyone reacted. She told me how Pamela had remained calm, and called her a respectable, strong, and patient women. When she finished, Idell dropped her chin and peered at me over her glasses.

"John, I don't know what you did to that woman—don't want to know—but if I was you, I'd do whatever it takes to get her back 'cause it'll be a long time before you find another one like her."

"I don't want another one 'like' her. I want Pamela."

She raised her eyebrows. "Well?"

I shrugged.

She humphed. "Just what I thought. You men are so damn good at messing up relationships, but you don't know squat about how to fix them."

Again, I had nothing to say. Pamela took care of everything: told her parents, forwarded my mail, and explained to Jackson why I was staying with Idell. I never found out what she told him, but whatever she said satisfied him and the only questions he asked when we were together concerned how I planned to feed him.

Aunt Idell let loose another disapproving grunt and shook her head.

With nothing to say, I stayed quiet. The week after the funeral, I wanted to go back to work, but Matt suggested I take more time off. He said losing a father is sometimes harder than we imagined it to be. He didn't know about my other loss.

"Take a few weeks and relax." He patted me on the back. "Call me when you feel ready, all right? Don't worry about a thing; you're still my Lucky John."

I drove back to Crown City and helped Bobby clear out Dad's clothes, tools, papers and all the other stuff related to the business. We also met with a lawyer who helped to transfer the business title to Bobby. Mom had gone to Ohio to visit with her family and left it all up to us. She separated the things she wanted to keep and told us to do whatever we wanted to do with the rest. The only thing I wanted was that log-cabin valet.

I had the place to myself after Bobby left in the evenings. Growing up, I always felt alone in that house but that was nothing compared to being alone. Nighttime was the worst. I stayed up as late as I could stand it because that little girl, or someone like her, kept showing up in my dreams, hands open and waiting. I never had anything to give her, and each night she would fade away looking sad and disappointed.

After three days of cleaning out, throwing away, and taking trips to the Goodwill drop-off center, Bobby told me he had to get back to the business of plumbing. I was alone the following day—no phone calls or neighbors stopping by. The next day was the same, and as I laid down for the night it dawned on me that I could have died without another soul knowing; my corpse, cold and rotting for days and days, until the stench floated out the windows and brought the neighbors over.

I drove back to Long Beach the next day.

•          •          •

Idell continued to stare at me. The silence between us was on the verge of becoming uncomfortable when she said, "Well, since you don't know what to do about this mess, just do what my daddy used to say: put some time on it."

A look of panic flashed across my face. Pamela and I separated three weeks ago, but it felt like months. I wasn't eager to put time on anything.

Idell read my face. "I know you're worried about your wife, which is good. You should be. But you need time to figure out just how much you want to stay married to her."

"I want to stay married to her."

"Watch your voice, boy." She studied me through her glasses, quiet and deep in thought. Then she said, "You through fooling around?"

I swallowed hard, squirmed in my seat, and couldn't seem to stop my eyes from darting around the room, trying to land on anything but Aunt Idell. She was the last person I'd expect to ask me that. She wasn't even on any of my who-knows lists. How could she know? What did she know?

"Well," she said after about a minute of silence. I met her eyes and saw my father looking back at me. Same round eyes, same dark brown irises, same thick eyebrows. I nodded.

"Yes ma'am," I said. "I'm through."

To my relief, Auntie didn't ask for any details like the whys or how comes. She knew just as well as I that there were no good answers to those questions. She only grunted and nodded her approval. "Good."

I leaned my head on the back of the sofa and stared at the ceiling. Her put time on it approach seemed like a big risk to me, but she was right. I definitely had no idea how to fix my marriage, so taking the wait and see approach seemed like my only option.

When I looked back at her, she was smiling. "It'll be kinda nice having you around again." Then she added, "Don't worry, son. That woman loves you. A lot." She settled back into her seat. "I've been around all different kinds of love in my life, and I can tell the real from the fake. I knew when you first brought her around here that she had it good for you. Just like I had it for my Jimmy, and just like Emily had it for Walter."

She got quiet again, and I could tell her mind was drifting back into the past. What or who she was thinking about wasn't hard to figure out. After half a minute she continued.

"I know my niece must have had some kinda love for her son. But maybe since her momma never showed her any love, she didn't know how. None of those no-good men she picked up ever loved her either. Not for long anyway." For the first time, I sensed a little resentment in her voice. She had always talked about

Precious with the same neutral tone Dad used—like they were talking about a piece of furniture or something.

I straightened up and asked to know more, anything. But she shook her head.

"No sense in bringing all that up. Your daddy and his momma have a chance to make their own peace now. Up there." She cast her eyes to the Heavens. When she looked back, her lips puckered together in concentration. Our eyes met. "And we down here can make peace too you know." Then she added: "And don't be a stubborn fool about it like you were the last time you got kicked out of your home."

• • •

Mom was in Ohio almost three weeks. When she came back, she bought all new bedroom furniture, repainted the inside of the house, and installed new carpet. She spends half her time in her craft room, the other half in her garden. She also joined a bridge club and is training to be a hospital volunteer that helps with the babies in the nursery.

Bobby goes to a grief support group once a week at the church. He also took a night class at the adult school and learned all about heating and air conditioning installation and repair, then renamed the business, Roberts Plumbing, Heating and Air Condition Service. Natalyn is very proud of him. All the worry between Bobby and Mom about each other's after turned out to be a big waste of time.

About five weeks after my father died, I went back to work, but spend the days doing cold-calls or following up on old leads. Ted and Lisa have become the new favored disciples of The Board and Matt Hudson. I see my son on weekends and one night a week. During our weekend time together, we usually go to visit my mom. Every time I see my wife, I ask her how she's doing and ask her to tell her family hello for me. She does the same. We're as cordial as two strangers on a bus.

That Sunday at church was the last time I saw Janet. I'll go by the drug store to see the twins, but always decline any other invitations. After a while, they stopped asking. Jeff did tell me that Janet decided to move to New York.

"She always liked it there," he told me. "After Mom took her that summer, that's all she talked about."

Kim was my last affair. She was true to her word and never called me again. I must have been emitting a loser vibe because the women that used to flock to me now treated me like the boy who always got picked last for basketball. Or maybe I just didn't see them anymore.

Lam Phuoc Foods, Inc. turned out to be our biggest contract of the year. Matt thanked me with another bonus, which I saved in a mutual fund. He keeps a wary eye on me and asks about once a week, "So, is my Lucky John back?"

"Not yet," I answer.

Not yet.

# The End

# Note from the Author

Word-of-mouth is crucial for any author to succeed. If you enjoyed *Lucky John*, please leave a review online—anywhere you are able. Even if it's just a sentence or two. It would make all the difference and would be very much appreciated.

Thanks!
Desiree

# About the Author

Desiree R. Kannel is a writer and educator from Southern California. Desiree discovered her love creative writing and storytelling while teaching writing to 4th grade students. She left education to pursue her MFA and now teaches creative writing to youth and adults through her workshop, Rose Writers. She is a founding board member of the Long Beach Literary Arts Center, and a chapter lead of Women Who Submit, an organization dedicated to empowering women writers to submit their work for publication.

Desiree's short stories have appeared in *Running Wild Press Short Story Anthology* and Escaped Ink's *Tall Tales & Short Stories*.

Thank you so much for reading one of our **Literary Fiction** novels.
If you enjoyed our book, please check out our recommendation
for your next great read!

*The Five Wishes of Mr. Murray McBride* by Joe Siple

2018 Maxy Award "Book Of The Year"
"A sweet...tale of human connection...
will feel familiar to fans of Hallmark movies."
*-Kirkus Reviews*

"An emotional story that will leave readers meditating on the
life-saving magic of kindness."
*-Indie Reader*

View other Black Rose Writing titles at
www.blackrosewriting.com/books and use promo code
PRINT to receive a **20% discount** when purchasing.

Made in the USA
Las Vegas, NV
27 November 2020

11595588R00099